A Body on the Shoreline

Other books by J.R. Seeger

MIKE4 Series

MIKE4
Friend or Foe
The Executioner's Blade
O'Connell's Treasure
A Graveyard for Spies
The Silicon Addiction
Playground for Ambition
The Swordfish of Deception

Steampunk Raj Series

A School for the Great Game
A Sound like Distant Thunder
The Enigma of Treason

A Body on the Shoreline

A WWII MYSTERY

J.R. Seeger

MISSION POINT PRESS

Readers are encouraged to go to www.MissionPointPress.com to contact the author or to find information on how to buy this book in bulk at a discounted rate.

Published by Mission Point Press
2554 Chandler Rd.
Traverse City, MI 49696
(231) 421-9513
www.MissionPointPress.com

ISBN: 978-1-961302-88-4 (Softcover)
ISBN: 978-1-965278-04-8 (Hardcover)
Library of Congress Control Number: 2024915978

Printed in the United States of America

*False face must hide
what the false heart doth know.*
William Shakespear,
Macbeth act 1, scene 7, line 82

TABLE OF CONTENTS

PROLOGUE — THE THIRD BOAT

12 October 1942, North shore of Lake Ontario

The commandos came out of the darkness and onto the north shore of the lake, wearing forest-green waxed cotton, black watch caps, and black wool gloves. Their canvas boots trod quietly across the shoreline pebbles as they waded onto the beach carrying the canvas-and-wood kayaks. Two men per kayak, the four men remained silent but relaxed.

They knew they were at the end of an eight hour exercise. It started as they slipped into the black waters of Lake Ontario, leaving the rusting hulk of a Great Lakes ore hauler that served as their mother ship. The task involved paddling surreptitiously along the shore near the General Motors plant and then landing at a beach marked by two small red-filtered torches. It had been a long night fighting both the current and the north winds of the lake. They were glad to be on land.

The spotlights caught them unawares. Suddenly, they were sur-rounded by men in Canadian Army uniforms, British Enfield rifles at port arms with bayonets reflecting the glare of the spotlights. In the darkness behind the lights, a voice on a loudspeaker said, "All right you men. Put down your boats and put up your hands."

The men looked at each other in amazement. Before they left, the chief instructor for small boat operations, Major Bill Brocker, had given them clear orders. Launch from the ship; paddle as close to the shore as possible; use a special, waterproof camera to photograph a Canadian plant making aircraft parts; avoid detection by the guards at the plant and the Canadian and US Coast Guard fast boats that patrolled the Great Lakes; and come ashore in darkness at 2230hrs. One of the men looked at the radium dial on his Elgin military watch. They were right on time. He paid for that check with a sharp rap from the butt of an Enfield rifle, driving him to his knees on the shoreline.

"I said, put up your hands. You are under arrest as saboteurs under the provisions of the War Powers Act of 1939." A second team of Canadian soldiers, this time military policemen, came up behind them, secured their hands with handcuffs and marched them away to a waiting Chevrolet lorry with canvas sides and back. In a few minutes, the men were in the truck and speeding back to Special Training School 103, known to everyone on site as Camp X. They would spend the rest of the night under a mock interrogation. While a surprise, they knew it was just another part of their Special Operations Executive. Every hardship in training might help save their lives when they were deployed into occupied Europe and behind Nazi lines.

As the staff picked up the two boats and loaded them into a second lorry, the senior instructor, a Scottish commando named Mackenzie, looked at his deputy and said, "Hamish, I know we dispatched six men. Where are the other two?"

"Major, I have no idea. I checked, and the patrol boats didn't see them. They clearly didn't come ashore with their mates. Once we get the four processed, I will know the names of the missing ones and we will start a search using our own safety boats."

Mackenzie nodded. "I already know at least one of them. It is that damned visitor, Fleming."

"The one from the Admiralty?"

"Exactly, Hamish. Admiral Godfrey's aide from Room 39. Fleming convinced the admiral that he needed to observe some of our training in case the Naval Intelligence Department wanted to create their own set of commandos for what Fleming called *special* missions."

"Not likely, sir. There are more than enough commandos, and special missions are precisely what we do. That's why we are here."

Mackenzie shook his head and took a few moments to light his pipe. The embers in the bowl of the pipe glowed in the darkness as the wind blew the smoke toward the lake. "Who knows, Hamish. We'd best find out what happened to that third boat."

"Sir, are you sure this is the best idea?"

The speaker was a Canadian with a strong Slavic accent. A Croatian émigré, Petyr Jovanovic was doing his best to simply survive the training and, with luck, return to Yugoslavia to fight the Nazis in his homeland. For certain, he did not want to go back to the Canadian destroyer where he had served until just a few weeks ago. The destroyer was an old Royal Canadian Navy warship from the Great War. It served as a poorly manned, poorly maintained coastal patrol vessel until 1939. After a quick and mostly unsuccessful refit, the ship joined convoy duty traveling from North American ports to ports on the English coast. His ship barely stayed afloat in the rough seas of the North Atlantic. When they had no protection from air patrols from either Newfoundland or England the convoys sailed a zigzag course, tempting the German U-boats to find them and sink them.

As a machinist mate, Jovanovic had spent his waking hours well below decks trying to keep the boilers running and the ship underway. He never knew what was happening on deck except for rare times when he pulled a deck watch manning an aft gun turret searching for the submarine he was certain would sink his ship. He found it all a terrifying way to serve his adopted country.

On his last shore leave in St. John's, he heard of the request for volunteers with European languages willing to apply for special service. He raised his hand, figuring no matter what the special services might be, they couldn't be worse than working below decks in a 40-year-old destroyer. In short order, he ended up in a training camp on the shore of Lake Ontario. While less terrifying than waiting for German torpedoes to crack the hull of his ship, the entry-level training for the special services was no picnic. And now, he was paddling a kayak on his own while his crewmate, a Royal Navy officer no less, was in the water swimming alongside the craft and dragging a dead body.

The officer raised his head above the water and said, "We can see the shore, Petyr, so it's not far. I'm fine so long as you keep paddling."

"Aye, aye, sir." Petyr had been working as Fleming's partner the last week. In his view, the Brit was well and truly crazy, but he had to admit, he was all in with the training. Royal Navy officers he had met in the past rarely spoke to men from "below decks." They ate in a separate mess, worked in separate stations on ships and left hard labor to the petty officers and seamen. This man, Ian Fleming, focused on the training as if his life depended on it. His classmates said Fleming worked at the Admiralty, so Petyr reckoned that unlike the rest of them Fleming probably wouldn't be involved in dangerous duty. Still, he carried his load without complaining and that was enough for Jovanovic.

Given his enthusiasm, when Fleming saw the dead body floating next to their boat Jovanovic wasn't surprised that Fleming rolled out of the boat and swam toward the body. Since he wasn't about to even try to explain to the instructors why he lost a Royal Navy officer in the cold waters of Lake Ontario, Jovanovic stayed next to Fleming as he pulled the body alongside their kayak and then swam toward shore.

As they came up on the beach the powerful spotlights switched on again, capturing them in their white-hot gaze. A loudspeaker voice said, "Fleming, why are you not with your teammates?"

Fleming pulled the body ashore while Jovanovic dragged the kayak. "Major Mackenzie, I believe we have a reasonable explanation. It would appear we have found a body."

Mackenzie was not about to be confounded by what he saw as a tourist to his training. He accepted that he had orders to allow Fleming to train with his men, but he was not well pleased that a staff officer was taking a training slot from someone who would eventually be sent behind enemy lines to kill Nazis. He had allowed Fleming to participate in this specific training only because Jovanovic's normal partner had been injured in an obstacle course the previous week. The exercise required six men in three boats. Mackenzie assigned Fleming as the sixth man in the third boat. Mackenzie did have another reason to assign Fleming to this training; he knew that the event was supposed to conclude with two hours of surprise interrogation. He thought it would serve the English toff right to spend a few hours in a cell. And now, here he was with a dead body.

Mackenzie turned to his deputy. "Hamish, sort this out. I have no patience for Fleming's flair for the dramatic." With that, he waved to the crew to shut down the lights. As the beach returned to darkness, he walked toward his jeep.

His subordinate spoke into the darkness: "Yes, sir."

The Investigation: Day One

14 October 1942

CHAPTER ONE — WHO IS THE VICTIM?

Royal Canadian Mounted Police Senior Staff Sergeant Miles Lundin was sitting at the counter of the St. George Street Diner mulling over his tea. Deke Kelly stood on the opposite side of the counter. He took his not-exactly-clean bar towel and wiped the surface in front of Lundin's mug of tea, hoping to get the Mountie's attention.

"Miles, are you going to order breakfast or not? It's closing in on six thirty and I know you must be at the barracks by eight." Lundin grumbled something that Kelly decided must be an order. He said, "Bacon, eggs, and toast, right?"

Following another grumble and a nod, Kelly turned to the grill and started up the meal. The bacon sizzled almost immediately and the eggs nearly scrambled themselves on the grill. Kelly opened the diner five days a week at 5:30 a.m. to catch Toronto's dockside crowd, and then kept busy through late breakfasts for the businessmen who wandered in after eight. He dropped the plate in front of his friend. "Now, eat the grub and tell me why you are even more grumpy than usual."

Lundin looked up from his tea and said only, "Thanks, Deke," as he began hesitantly to eat his meal. Eggs first, then he used the toast to make a bacon sandwich. Finally, he said, "You remember Jacoby? Our old mate from the Canadian Royal Rifles in France?"

Deke tapped his artificial leg with the grill spatula, making a hollow, wooden sound. "How could I forget? You and Jacoby pulled me out of the trench, wrapped a tourniquet below my knee and saved my life. I got shipped home and you two stayed on into the occupation of Germany. What about him?"

"I just got a note from his wife. He died in Hong Kong. Defending the city."

"Jesus, Mary and Joseph, Miles! We are losing them left and right."

"I should be there, Deke."

Deke shook his head. "You should be right here doing what you do. We both spent our time with the Regiment in the last war. Jacoby was a good five years younger than either of us, and didn't exactly prove to be a model citizen after the war. I think he was about one step away from prison and two steps away from his creditors when he enlisted the second time. His wife will be gutted now, but the last time I saw him he said she had a knife to his throat. I'm sorry he was killed, but that certainly isn't your fault."

"It's not right. Friends dying over there, protecting the country, while I'm home pushing paper. I could have helped him."

"And, just maybe, I would have heard from some other pal that you were dead. You are a Mountie for god's sake! Protecting the Dominion. There are plenty of villains here who have tried to kill you, and you either put them in the ground or in prison. Plenty more out there."

"It's like throwing rocks in the lake, Deke. Always more."

"But who is going to protect a geezer like me if you don't? You've been keeping an eye on me since we were in grade school."

Lundin nodded, unable to shake the dark mood. What had over 20 years of his life in the Force done for him? He looked at his empty plate and finished his tea. "I suppose keeping you safe is worth something."

"That's the spirit! Now, get out of here. I've got respectable people coming in soon and they don't want to see a mug like you capitalizing on good diner geography. And, just in case you are interested, you stink."

Lundin nodded. "I just came from the Queensbury. Did a workout with the Tunneys. You never know when you might need to punch a guy's lights out."

"Or, learn to take a punch and then punch back."

Lundin stood up, grabbed his red-and-black checked hunting jacket off the coat hook and pulled it over his sweatsuit. The clock above the door showed 6:45. The barracks at 136 Beverley was only a five-minute walk away. It was definitely time for him to use the barracks shower and pull his uniform out of his locker. He was a disciplined man. He had been at his desk in the Toronto Barracks at 7:50 every morning since he arrived from his assignment in the Northwest Territories. He wasn't about to miss that deadline. He turned to his pal and said, "Keep the change, Deke."

Deke had already swept up the five Canadian dollars. "Next time we see each other, I want to know why you aren't married, yet," he said.

Lundin smiled as he opened the diner door. "Just lucky I guess."

Lundin was at his desk nursing another cup of tea. He was thinking about what Deke Kelly had said about keeping the Dominion safe. Twenty years in the Mounted Police Force had filled his once-fit body with the aches and pains of a middle-aged man. He had scars on his arms and along his ribcage from knife fights in rural Canada. His nose had been broken too many times to count. He was missing two toes on his right foot from frostbite during service in the Canadian North. Every morning his body reminded him of these injuries and every time he walked, he did his best to disguise the limp caused by his missing toes. Worse still, every minute he sat behind a desk in the Toronto offices reminded him of how he hated paperwork. He had fought hard to re-enlist and deploy with the Regiment, but the RCMP would not release him.

After losing the battle to return to his regiment, in the spring of

1942 Lundin volunteered for selection for an RCMP provost unit headed to England with the First Canadian Division. Again, no luck. His commander insisted that Lundin's experience was needed in protecting the Dominion. What Lundin heard instead was, "You're too old, Miles."

Some days he did feel old, but not so old that he couldn't fight for his country. With the world at war, law enforcement on the homefront seemed like a distraction. There would always be villains willing to prey on the weak; the Force served as the most powerful entity providing safety and order to all Canadians. But, as he said to Kelly, it seemed to him like throwing rocks at Lake Ontario. It hardly mattered to the lake no matter how many rocks you threw in.

His recent work out of the RCMP Toronto barracks focused on the same sort of villainy that he faced before the war: murders, especially murders of government officials or in the Native tribes, and theft of government property. In the past year, his only challenging case involved the theft of 20 Lee-Enfield rifles from an Ontario police armory. After a few weeks, he had arrested both the thieves and a smuggler planning to sell the weapons in Ireland. No saboteurs or Nazi spies to be seen. Every day since he closed that case, Lundin made the argument to his sergeant major that the Ontario Provincial Police could easily handle that type of work. He wanted something tangible that he could say was defending the Dominion. And nearly every day, his sergeant major told him the same thing: "Lundin, focus on your job and stop moaning."

The phone rang at his desk. The secretary for the Chief Inspector was on the line. "Miles," she said, "the boss wants to see you."

Lydia Mansfield was the only person in the barracks who regularly called him by his first name. She was old enough to be his mother, and there were some in the barracks who joked she was old enough to remember when the RCMP was called the Northwest Mounted Police. Lundin liked her and appreciated that she was unfailingly friendly when he visited the front office of the old Victorian mansion turned into a police barracks. It was the only thing that made a trip to the Chief Inspector's office in any way pleasant.

As he walked down the hallway, he buttoned his brown tunic. One simply did not walk into the Chief Inspector's office in a shirt and tie. His polished brown boots rattled the wood planking. Both junior officers and the administrative staff stayed well clear as Lundin limped past. They saw one of the legends of the Force heading toward the seniors' office and they certainly didn't want to get in the way of what must be an important new case. They had no idea why this giant (over six feet tall) with his close-cropped greying hair, permanently tanned skin, and hooked nose was heading to the Chief Inspector, but Lundin didn't look well pleased. His grey-blue eyes were focused on the door at the end of the hallway, and no one along the corridor intended to get in his way.

He stopped at Lydia's desk. She nodded and he approached the oak door with the crest of the RCMP above a panel in gold lettering that read *Chief Inspector.* He knocked three times. A voice from the other side of the door shouted, "ENTER!"

Lundin opened the door and walked up to the desk. "Sir, you wanted to see me?"

Chief Inspector George McClellan was the senior Mountie in the Toronto region. He was a large, fit man from Saskatchewan, who looked the part when called upon for political duties wearing his scarlet parade-ground tunic, polished black boots and Stetson hat. He was a plain-spoken man of the prairie and a tough disciplinarian known for his no-nonsense manner. He had worked his way up the Force the same way as Lundin, from distant outposts in the North to regional barracks and now to the Toronto barracks. Lundin thought he was the perfect boss and likely to be head of the RCMP before long. Today, he was in a white shirt and tie with his blue uniform jacket hanging from a nearby coat hook. Behind him on the wall was a large maple wood crest of the RCMP and a picture of the king; his red-serge dress uniform was on a coat rack just to the left of the King's portrait. McClellan looked up at Lundin, who stood at attention.

He passed a piece of paper and a pen to Lundin. "Miles, I need you to sign this before we go any farther." Lundin was surprised to be addressed by his given name. The chief inspector had previously only used his last name or, more often, just his rank. The paper had the formal crest of the Dominion, as expected, but he had not expected to see the formal crest of the United Kingdom nor the title of the next line: Official Secrets Act 1911.

Lundin read the paragraphs below the title which listed the penalties for revealing Crown secrets and the last paragraph, which said:

The signatory takes these obligations freely with the full understanding that any information that he acquires or receives during this operation will be considered most secret. Penalties for release of this information will be based on the above list.

Below that last paragraph was a signature block with his full name and rank: Miles Andrew Lundin. Senior Staff Sergeant, RCMP. Below his name were two further lines for witnesses, and those two typed signature blocks were for the chief inspector and Sergeant Major James Tyle, who was, as in all military organizations, the man who made sure things were accomplished on time and to standard.

The chief inspector and Sergeant Major Tyle watched as he signed the paper. He passed the document back to McClellan, who signed and passed it to Tyle, who signed it as well. Tyle placed the document in a paper folder and sealed it with an RCMP stamp and a second stamp marked Most Secret, then placed it in the oak tray on the chief inspector's desk marked OUT. Lundin had been on a fair number of sensitive investigations in his career, but this was a first. He had no idea what it meant.

McClellan said, "Miles, have a seat. This protocol was demanded by the other entities of this investigation. We are complying with the direct request of the office of the Prime Minister in Ottawa. While the secrecy agreement is clear, what is not yet clear to us is why we needed this protocol. Perhaps as you proceed, it will be clearer."

Lundin had no idea what to say, so he chose to say nothing. The chief inspector continued, "In the meantime, I wanted you to know that regardless of anything else, whatever you do in this new investigation you do for the Crown, but you only report to the two of us. No one else."

Lundin thought for a moment before he spoke. He had been in the chief inspector's office several times, usually at the end of an investigation or for a promotion of one of the Toronto team. His usual point of contact was the sergeant major. The last time he was in the office was to receive a long-delayed award for work in a previous assignment in the Northwest Territories. Clearly, he needed to proceed with caution. "Sir, I absolutely accept the conditions. What exactly is the investigation?"

Tyle took over the discussion. His voice had the sound of gravel rolling out of a dump truck. Lundin suspected that his own voice would sound the same after another ten years in the Force. "We have a dead Canadian named Edward Novak, also known as Ned Novak. He was working at a military camp on Lake Ontario. It is a secret base, created in December 1941 after the Japanese attacked the Americans in Pearl Harbor and the Commonwealth Forces across Asia."

McClellan took over. "I went up there when they were first building the place. The briefing was vague, but it is a training camp for Canadians and Americans who are going to be spies and saboteurs. Mostly, it is a ramshackle set of buildings surrounded by farmland. Perhaps perfect isolation for what they are trying to accomplish. I assume Novak was involved in the training."

Tyle continued, "We checked Novak's background. Born in Yugoslavia and came to Canada with his parents after the Great War. Both parents are dead. No other family to speak of except a sister in Vancouver. He doesn't have a wife or children. Before the war, he worked on lake freighters. Volunteered for service in 1939. Served with the Canadian Navy. Disappeared from the public records in 1940. Now, we find out he was working at this camp since December 1941."

McClellan looked at his sergeant major and then returned his gaze to Lundin. "We hope the officers at the camp cooperate with your investigation. But I don't expect much help. The last time I visited the camp and received an official tour, they were polite but offered no answers to any of my questions about the training. I thought the Force efforts at tracking Nazi spies might benefit from the training. They seemed disinterested in any counter-espionage training." McClellan looked over at his sergeant major.

Tyle continued, "There are plenty of secrets out there, and they don't much like outsiders asking questions. In this case of a murdered Canadian, they have been most secret and, mark my words, it will get even worse the closer you get to the truth. There may be something embarrassing happening at the camp, or it just might be a classic case of annoying bureaucracy. I don't know much other than this is a murder in Canadian territory. That makes it our murder case. Do what you must to get to the bottom of it."

Lundin thought for a moment. He also demanded clarity in his investigations. "Sir, do I cooperate with them? What I mean is normally you are my chain of command, and I usually work with a member of the Crown prosecution office and ignore anyone else who claims to have authority. Are any of these officers in my chain of command?"

McClellan was adamant. "No. You work for the Force, and that means you are working inside our authorities. Do not let any of these British officers prevent you from doing your job. I will need a daily report. You can call by telephone, or if it is too sensitive you can drive back down to Toronto and we will talk it through. Never forget, Novak was a loyal Canadian who was killed on Canadian soil and dumped into Lake Ontario. He may have been killed because of his job, or he may have been killed for other reasons. Find the answers and then we will work to prosecute the perpetrators. Clear?"

Lundin nodded to his commander and checked with his sergeant major. Tyle handed Lundin the thin case file and motioned to the door. Lundin saluted and walked out of his commander's office with absolutely no clue as to what to expect.

Lundin sat at his desk. He was back in his shirt sleeves, a cup of tea in his left hand and his Parker fountain pen in his right. He was taking notes in the leather field notebook that was with him day and night. It had become as much a part of him as his uniform and his Colt sidearm. The case file was just a few pages. The first page offered what little the administrative staff could find on the victim. Novak was 35 years old. Medium build, brown hair, blue eyes. He had been a resident of St. Catherines, working the lake freighters. Page two had Novak's certification as a radio communicator for Great Lakes shipping and a copy of his union card issued in 1932 with the Canadian Merchant Service Guild. Page three had manifest listings for the last five routes before the war. He worked primarily on iron ore freighters traveling from Thunder Bay to the steel mills on Lake Erie. No disciplinary problems, and only one promotion from 1932 to 1939. Union dues paid in full through the end of 1942.

The next page captured Novak's military service. He joined the Canadian Navy in 1939. The Navy photo showed a man in the Navy recruit uniform wearing a white service cap. Canadian Navy records offered few details other than his rating — radioman third class. There were no details on what ships he served on or how he ended up at a camp on Lake Ontario. There were no orders assigning him to the camp in Oshawa. Lundin had reviewed military files before — usually after some seaman or soldier was found dead in Toronto. He had never seen a personnel file so empty of information. Was this simply because of Novak's rank, or because someone purged the file before it was sent to the RCMP? He expected that would be a question for later in the investigation. Perhaps more secrets than even the Chief Inspector considered.

The final set of pages were the coroner's report. Lundin had not expected much. Most coroners he met in rural Canada were country doctors who signed death certificates. Knife and gunshot wounds were easy to detect and reported on the death certificate. Other than that the death certificate usually stated "failure to thrive," which could mean a dread disease, a heart attack or even something more sinister but hard to detect, such as poisoning or smothering.

In this case, the report was exceptionally detailed; five pages including photos of the body and several notes. Two of the photos linked to the notes stated clearly: *Novak did not drown.* The coroner offered a broken neck as the likely cause of death. Lundin decided he needed to talk to this coroner: Dr. James Sutton, Captain, Royal Navy, retired. 9420 King's Road, Oshawa.

"This is a man who knows his business," Lundin said to himself. "Tomorrow is going to be a busy day."

The Investigation: Day Two

15 October 1942, Camp X near Oshawa, Ontario

CHAPTER TWO —
A MOST SECRET PLACE

The drive from Toronto to Oshawa the next morning was tedious. Not that it was a long way. Rather, King's Highway #2 was a badly paved road that snaked northeast out of Toronto along the lakeshore. The potholes and cracked asphalt forced Lundin to keep his speed well below the posted limit of 45mph. Lundin suspected that the road had last been paved just before the Great Depression hit Canada. The country had little available funds, and those funds went to keeping Canadians fed. Lundin would also be the first to admit that few Canadians had the luxury of a car as nice as his assigned black Buick patrol car. It was built for speed, but luckily the long-nosed vehicle also had a good suspension, so the washboard and ruts of the highway did little harm to either car or driver.

The route took him through farm fields and a few windbreaks of poplar and maples turning golden in the fall. Lundin had to keep his mind on driving and could not use the time to design a strategy for his initial steps in the investigation. As the drive wore on, he realized that he would have to spend at least one night either at this camp or in Oshawa if he intended to get anything done on his first day. This was hardly a problem. He always traveled with a leather kit bag with his field gear, a sweater, several changes of underwear and socks, a shaving kit and shoe polish for his boots. In the trunk of the Buick, he had a pair of rubber farm boots, in case there was wading to be done, and a Winchester pump shotgun known as a trench gun in case his Colt was insufficient firepower. For now, there wasn't enough information, and he knew the first day was always the most important in an investigation, so he wanted to get started as soon as possible.

When he finally pulled up to the main gate, he saw two young Canadian privates sitting in a guard house behind a white and red striped metal barrier across the driveway. He stopped and waited for one of the two soldiers to come to his car. When they did not seem interested in doing their job, Lundin gave a toot on the car horn. When that did not stir them, he got out of the car and prepared to give these young men a lesson in military discipline. At well over six feet, six inches tall in his boots and Stetson, wearing his RCMP brown tunic with the crown and stripes sewn on the sleeve, Lundin expected a degree of respect. So far, he had received none. The gate guards were young men who didn't seem to care at all that they were addressing someone senior in rank or a man who could easily break them into small pieces before they knew what hit them. They just refused to raise the gate.

Lundin was well on his way to deciding which of the two men he would harm first when a jeep raced up to the guard house. A man wearing what looked like an amalgam of different service uniforms got out of the jeep. Even before reaching the gate house, he gave the gate guards a dressing down and ordered them to begin doing press-ups until he told them to stop. That made Lundin feel some-what better. The newly arrived man lifted the gate himself and walked over to Lundin.

Over his years as a Mountie, Lundin had learned to quickly size up men. It was part of his job, and it was how he stayed alive. As the man approached, Lundin reviewed him from head to toe. The first thing he noticed was this man in his late thirties carried himself more like an athlete than a ramrod-straight British officer. Light on his feet with arms swinging gently at his sides. Not the walk of a man beaten early on into military formality, and certainly not an officer created at Sandhurst. He was wearing a forest green beret with no regimental insignia, and there was no rank showing on his uniform. He wore an olive green wool sweater, heavy wool brown trousers and well-worn, rough-polished brown boots. Sewn on the left shoulder of his sweater was a blue serge patch with red stitching of an anchor, a set of wings and a Tommy gun. Over that patch was sewn a curved blue stripe with red stitching that said *commando*.

Lundin decided here was a man who had faced hardship, perhaps at war but also in life before the war. A man who earned respect rather than demanding it. Based on his assessment, Lundin came to the position of attention and saluted the man. After he received a salute in return, he was offered a handshake. "Senior Staff Sergeant, I apologize for the nitwits at the gate. My name is Hamish Creed, a captain serving in this lunatic asylum for my previous sins. And, just so you know, we don't follow the King's regulations at the camp. This is the last salute you should expect to receive. Officers and enlisted are all treated the same…badly, if you want to know the truth." Creed smiled at Lundin and then said, "Please follow me to the headquarters building and we'll sort out why you are here."

Creed walked back to his jeep, did a quick reverse turn, and headed along the road toward the largest building on the compound. As he followed through the gate, Lundin smiled at the sight of the two guards still doing press-ups. Lundin wondered if Creed had simply forgotten to tell the guards to stop or whether he just didn't care if they weren't clever enough to stop after he left. As he drove into the compound, he noticed it looked like many of the new military posts throughout Canada. They were all thrown together from any available materials and didn't appear to be built to last. He remembered the chief inspector used the term ramshackle. Lundin agreed. He had seen more than his share of remote government outposts in his years with the RCMP, and this one looked like most villages in the north. Temporarily permanent with signs of neglect.

Creed was waiting at the door of the headquarters building and led Lundin past a young soldier serving at the entrance control point. Lundin had been prepared for another confrontation, but the soldier looked terrified of both Creed and the Mountie who followed him down the hall. At the end of the main hall, they turned right and walked past four doors before coming to an open door. Creed turned and said, "Welcome to my little garret."

Lundin walked into the room, finding Creed had not exaggerated. It was no more than eight feet square with a desk, two chairs, a map table covered with maps and a bookcase filled with books. Lundin was a large man and he immediately worried he might knock something over if he wasn't careful. Creed said, "Wait just a tick and I'll get us some tea." He walked out, leaving the door open.

Lundin found a coat stand and put his Stetson on one of the hooks, unbuckled his Sam Brown belt and hung his gun belt and then his tunic on the coat stand. As he rolled up the sleeves of his uniform shirt, Lundin said to no one in particular, "If we are going to be informal, I suppose informal it shall be." He sat down and waited. Creed returned in a few minutes with a small tray with mugs of tea and a plate of tea biscuits.

"I'm glad you have accepted my invitation. If we must waste our time, the least we can do is be comfortable." He paused and placed the tray on his desk. "First, tea. How do you take it?"

Lundin said, "Black, one sugar."

"Done. And would you mind if I call you by your given name? It will be rather awkward if I have to say Senior Staff Sergeant Lundin every time we change a subject."

Lundin smiled and said, "It's Miles."

Creed smiled back and said, "Oh, we already know that, Miles. I was just being polite. You see, we selected you from the Force for this job. We needed a local man we can trust. Someone who wouldn't make too much of a fuss about a drowned man, but who could produce a report that everyone would accept. Did a bit of digging and found you. Then we had Mr. Stephenson reach out directly to Commissioner Wood to make sure you would be our man. Commissioner Wood seems to hold you in high regard, and that was good enough for Mr. Stephenson and for our camp commander, Lieutenant Colonel Brooker."

"Mr. Stephenson?"

"Miles, I suppose it's time to introduce you to some of our secrets. More tea?"

Lundin nodded. He looked out the window and saw the afternoon light fading to grey. He had hoped to start the investigation immediately and, instead, was having tea with a mysterious officer. He took his newly filled mug and said, "Hamish, I'm all ears."

Creed smiled. "Excellent. Well, let's start with where you are. The formal name is Special Training Site 103 or STS 103 for short. Most of the locals and just about all the staff simply call it Camp X. We are a facility that serves as a selection and training facility for an organization known as the Special Operations Executive."

"Some sort of military outfit like the Commandos?"

"Well, not exactly. First, we are not part of the War Ministry. Apparently, the Prime Minister decided that the various services were too conventional for what he had in mind. In London, they jokingly call us the Ministry of Ungentlemanly Warfare. In truth, SOE is part of the Ministry of Economic Warfare. A bit amusing, no?" Creed stopped to sip his tea. "I don't suppose you have heard of William Stephenson?"

Lundin gave Creed a cold look. "Absolutely. He was a Canadian ace in the Great War, returned and became an inventor and a millionaire. You might as well ask me if I know the name of the Governor General."

Creed raised his hands in mock surrender. "Apologies for that. Most of the Brits here have no idea who William Stephenson was. They only know what Mr. Stephenson is." He paused to sip his tea. "Well, when this war started, the British Secret Intelligence Service asked him to serve as their man in the Western Hemisphere. He works out of New York. Sometimes with the Yanks on all sorts of projects, sometimes on his own. We know he does more than his share of independent operations south of the American border."

"Spying?"

"Some, but also special missions to disrupt Nazi operations in the States and in South America. Sabotage and subversion. And, he has a close working relationship with another hero from the Great War, an American named Donovan. Donovan is the commander of the American version of the SOE, they call it the Office of Strategic Services. And, Mr. Stephenson is far more interested in what we do here than any bureaucratic work he might be conducting in either New York or Washington."

Lundin had a low tolerance for bureaucracy. He decided to cut to the chase. "What does this have to do with Novak?"

Creed paused and said, "I am getting there, Miles. I think you will need this context to understand something about the drowning. To be blunt, we train Canadians and Americans in sabotage, subversion and espionage. I understand the Yanks are building their own camps near Washington, DC so by next year we will be focused exclusively on your countrymen. Still, it is a joint project creating new members of a secret army. And, that secret army conducts operations in Nazi-occupied Europe. No uniforms, no reinforcements, and very few supplies. The men and women we train are going to risk their lives on their own. The centerpiece of this camp is secrecy. Secrecy will save their lives once they are behind the lines in Europe."

"They must be mad."

"Indeed, we are mad. And, yes, I was an early one. After my first mission, I barely made it out alive with the Gestapo hunting me. I was picked up by one of our motor torpedo boats at the last minute. I am still on the Gestapo most wanted list, so a return to Europe is unlikely to be in my future. I was reassigned to the SOE training facilities. Now, I train them here so they don't make the mistakes I made."

Lundin remained skeptical of the long story and the hospitality. He simply asked, "And?"

"Well, we would like the camp and our activities to remain secret. An accidental drowning at the camp made public might make the newspapers in Toronto or, worse still, New York. Honestly, the camp commander simply wants this resolved as quietly as possible."

Lundin had worked on sensitive political projects in Toronto and Winnipeg in the past. Politicians always wanted cases solved as quietly as possible. And, he found it curious that Creed remained committed to the term drowning rather than what Lundin knew to be the truth. Novak was murdered. It was too early to reveal what he knew to a man he had met only a few minutes before, so he decided to play along with the fiction. "So, who was the victim? Was he one of your students?"

"Well, no …"

"More secrets?"

"Oh, many more secrets, Miles. That's why you are here."

CHAPTER THREE —
EVEN MORE SECRETS

Creed stood and invited Lundin over to the map table. He pushed a map of Yugoslavia to the floor and focused his attention on the remaining sheet. Lundin recognized almost immediately that it was a map of the camp. Creed turned the map so that Lake Ontario was at the top and the road from Toronto was at the bottom.

"We have three different missions here," Creed said. "We are a selection program that determines if Canadian volunteers match our requirements. In that regard, we have been very lucky. Our interest has been in native speakers for our target countries in Europe, and Canada has many immigrants from those nations. If they make it through our month-long selection we send them to other SOE training in Britain, and eventually they are dispatched to the Continent. There is no guarantee that they will pass the other training programs, but so far our classes have provided dozens of men and women working behind enemy lines."

"Women?"

"The Nazis are blind to the idea that we use women. And, honestly, women tend to be far better radio operators than men. Resilience and communications skills are far more important for operations behind the lines than body mass or strength. These are men and women who work in the shadows." Creed said no more, and Lundin decided that this was all he was going to get out of the SOE officer.

"Now, our training includes small arms, explosives, hand-to-hand combat and small boat operations. We mix all of this with physical training and some psychological assessments. We even conduct mock interrogations to see how the students hold up. It is a very hard month." As he explained the training, Creed pointed to various parts of the camp. Lundin noted that there was another building not identified.

"Hamish, what's that building?"

"That is another of our secrets. It is called HYDRA, and it is a communications center that serves a most critical role in the war. It is a secure communications channel between Stephenson in New York and both SOE and SIS in London. There is talk to use HYDRA to open other lines of communication between London and Washington, perhaps even a direct line between Prime Minister Churchill and President Roosevelt. Think of it as a secure telephone switch between the UK and the US."

"Why here?"

"Why not here? I suspect you noticed we are not especially interesting from the outside. The nearest town is Oshawa, where there is a single General Motors factory, and we are surrounded by farms and farmers. Not the place you would expect to find an important radio communications center, eh? The wireless communications travel from England to here, and then by telex from here through Toronto and Buffalo to New York. No transatlantic cable needed for these communications."

Lundin was beginning to understand why he had signed the Official Secrets Act paperwork. He said, "So, you train spies and saboteurs, you serve as a private line between London and New York, and eventually between London and Washington. What else do you do?"

"We are beginning to train American and Canadian counter-espionage officers on the fine art of catching enemy agents, interrogating them and, ideally, turning them into double agents."

Lundin nodded. "What does this have to do with the victim?"

"Miles, the problem we face right now is this is a camp of trained killers. We need them to focus on their future jobs and we don't need any distractions, including a major investigation on what the camp commander sees as a simple drowning. People drown in Lake Ontario all the time. Novak was a HYDRA communicator. He might have been drunk. He might have had a fight with one of his HYDRA mates. We don't know and, honestly, we don't care. We just want this to be handled with discretion and prevent it from damaging our program, which is so important to our fight against the Nazis. We need this to be resolved quietly and as quickly as possible. It has nothing to do with our side of the camp. Now, what it might have to do with the secret communications center, none of us here know for sure."

Lundin let out a low whistle. "Not good."

"Miles, definitely not good."

CHAPTER FOUR — THE CRIME SCENE

undin thought that for all his hospitality, Creed was doing his best to distract his attention. Plus, it seemed most curious that this officer did not know (or at least did not want to admit) that Novak was killed and then thrown in the lake. Lundin needed further information from his host, but first he wanted to see the crime scene. In his previous murder investigations, the location usually provided the most critical context for solving the crime. It sounded simple, but it was by no means simplistic. There would always be something in the venue that helped explain the crime. In previous investigations, the act was usually the result of too much alcohol, too much money, or some petty jealousy. He wasn't sure what he would find in this den of spies and saboteurs, but he needed to start somewhere and that somewhere was always the crime scene.

To open the way to the crime scene, he said, "Hamish, tell me what you know about Novak."

Creed said, "I'm really a trainer here, so I knew precious little about the communicators at HYDRA. I will introduce you to his supervisor, Ken Stevens. What I know for certain is Novak was considered an excellent wireless operator. Novak was one of the early operators who helped set up the wireless center and was a shift supervisor at HYDRA. It is a twenty-four-hour operation, and he was the night supervisor."

"Perhaps we should see Mr. Stevens, and I would like to see where

Novak worked." Lundin paused. He decided to see how Creed would react. "And, obviously, I would like to see the crime scene."

Creed sucked air through his teeth. "Well, that might be a problem. You see, we really don't know where he drowned. As you probably already know, he was found floating in Lake Ontario just offshore."

"Who was the first one to handle the body?"

"Now that is something I can answer. We have a medical staff here at the camp, and they did a thorough investigation. Then they passed it on to the local coroner."

"Dr. Sutton. I have read his report."

For the first time in their discussion, Creed looked worried. "I didn't know the coroner had reported to the RCMP."

"Hamish, the coroner reports to the Crown Prosecutor and the Force is the investigative arm of that office. We got the full report."

"I haven't seen the coroner's report, but our team said he drowned and was in the water less than a day. So, he must have fallen in the lake right after his shift."

Lundin nodded. This was another line of inquiry. The camp medical staff should have easily seen that Novak had a broken neck, yet they had not reported it. Lundin knew full well how easy it was to kill a man. He had been forced to do so three times in his career. Only once did he use his service revolver. The other two had been hand-to-hand combat with violent men who had already killed others and had intended to kill him. Some parts of the human body were remarkably robust, while others were quite fragile. The neck and the skull were particularly vulnerable. The wrong punch, a blow to the side of the head or even a fall, and a man's life was gone. This British officer had said he was in a camp full of killers-in-training who would know the vulnerabilities of a man. That was not encouraging.

Lundin decided to push Creed again. "So, you don't know where he died?"

Creed shook his head. "Not a clue, Miles. Could have been one of several docks we have on the lake."

"And I don't suppose you have any idea who had a beef with Novak?"

"We need to talk to Ken."

"Then, let's talk to Ken."

"Well, he's on the night shift now that Novak is … Probably makes sense to catch him when he wakes up and heads to work."

Lundin wasn't sure if this was a delaying tactic or a legitimate argument. He said, "When does Novak's supervisor start his shift?"

"1800hrs."

Lundin looked at his trusted Elgin steel wristwatch. It was called a trench watch, though he hadn't worn a watch in the trenches. He didn't have the money to buy a watch during the war. His father had given him the Elgin when he joined the Mounties. It was a simple steel watch with fixed wire lugs as keepers that held a brown leather pass-through strap. He had worn it for nearly 20 years through ice and snow, gunfights and bar fights. It was the most precious personal item he owned. The watch showed 1620hrs. "Any other witnesses?"

"Now that's where I can help. The two men who recovered Novak's body are here as trainees at the camp." This time it was Creed who looked at his wristwatch, a British army issue timepiece that Lundin knew was called simply an ATP watch, standing for Army Trade Pattern, made by multiple British watchmakers. A simple white-faced watch with blued hands. It was easy to read, and Lundin assumed probably as rugged as his Elgin. "They should be finishing with their firearms training right now. We could meet them."

Lundin stood up, walked to the coat tree, pulled on his tunic and pistol belt, strapped down the Sam Browne belt and recovered his Stetson. "No time like the present, Hamish."

CHAPTER FIVE — THE HOUSE OF HORRORS

As Creed drove them to the firearms range, Lundin expected a traditional firing range. His experience both in the Force and in the Canadian Army had been the same: an open field with a berm at the far end, usually 200 to 300 yards away. Targets were placed at varying distances for rifle and pistol fire. In a traditional range, a series of firing positions would be marked by numbered stakes. Rifle firing took place in three positions: standing, seated and prone, with targets at 100, 200 and 300 yards. Pistol firing was conducted standing with the pistol extended at arm's length, engaging targets set up at 20, 50 or 100 feet. In all cases, the targets were paper bullseye targets with numbered rings.

Instead, Creed drove them to a narrow building, 40 yards long, with a long porch around all four sides. Lundin thought it looked more like a warehouse than any training structure. He could see there was a single narrow door at the entrance, and as they pulled up he heard pistol shots echoing from inside the building. He saw an individual leaving the building from an equally small door at the opposite end. He was dressed in an olive green jumpsuit with a white two-digit number painted on the back. As soon as the student, number 08, exited the building, an instructor met him and took control of the pistol. After they both removed cotton from their ears, they walked together away from the building to a seating area nearby. Lundin could see the instructor was giving the student feedback in a blunt and vigorous style.

Creed said, "Welcome to the House of Horrors."

"Eh?"

"The facility was designed by one of our SOE instructors named Fairbairn. Former Shanghai police officer who created a special task force to handle the Chinese gangs in the city in the 1930s. He designed this training facility based on work he was doing in SOE facilities in England and brought a pair of his cronies with him. They support his training agenda: Teach the students how to shoot to kill and to do so as fast and as accurately as possible. He calls his training 'shooting to live.' The students call the facility the house of horrors. Inside the building, there are multiple targets that pop up along the length of the building. Some are civilians, some have images of allied troops and some of Nazis. When the Nazi targets pop out from the wall or a doorway or the floor, there are also fireworks that go off seconds later. One instructor controls the targets and one instructor watches from outside the building through the windows you can see along the way. The students must place two rounds in the enemy targets when they pop up."

"It looks dangerous for the participants and the instructors."

"I suppose it could be, but we believe the risk is worth the reward of keeping these men and women alive." Creed pointed to the end of the building. "There is one of our female trainees coming out now." A thin woman, looking almost like an adolescent in her ill-fitting jumpsuit, walked out and met the instructor. He recovered the small automatic pistol and they walked to the seating area. As she walked away Lundin noticed her number, 010.

"The male student had a Colt .45 automatic, but the female student who just exited had a smaller Browning. And the female student has three digits on her back. Is that because she is a woman?"

Creed smirked. "Two questions there. First, all students must go through the House of Horrors with a Colt automatic, a smaller Browning automatic and a Colt Commando revolver." He pointed to the women sitting down on the bench.

"010 had already finished the session with the Colt and went through with the Browning. Students must score five out of six kills in each pass with no shots into friendly targets. So far, no one has completed the full three sessions at the first go."

Lundin did a quick calculation. If they had six possible targets to engage, with two rounds per target, they would have more targets than they would have bullets. "They have to do a reload inside the house?"

"Part of the training. If they see a civilian target, they can enter that alcove and reload. They must remember how many rounds they have fired so that they can get through the house with ammunition to spare. If they exit with an empty firearm, they start again. The instructor cadre are very strict about this." Creed continued, "Now, to your second question. The numbers on the back of the boiler suits, or coveralls as you North Americans call them, are so we can determine who is who when we are doing firearms and hand-to-hand combat training. Easier than trying to remember names and faces. Regular SOE recruits are given two-digit numbers. Officer trainees are given three-digit numbers. The woman you just saw, Beatrice Thomas, came from ATA."

"ATA?"

"Air Transport Auxiliary. Female pilots who fly aircraft manufactured in North America to England. Some are British pilots, some Commonwealth fliers. 010 is a Canadian. She was injured in a landing accident in England and returned to Canada. She wanted to continue to serve. We figured anyone willing to fly alone in a bomber across the North Atlantic was brave enough to do just about anything."

"Fair enough." While interesting, and although 010 looked to be quite attractive, Lundin wanted to keep his mind on the job. "Where are the men who found Novak?"

"You saw one of them when we first pulled up." He pointed over to the seating area to their left. "08 is named Petyr Jovanovic. Yugoslav emigre. Good chap. Another Canadian sailor like Novak."

"Is he indeed?"

"I thought you might find that interesting. We don't have many sailors here. Mostly either direct recruits or Canadian soldiers who volunteer while on leave."

"And the other?"

"An odd duck, to be sure. His name is Fleming, Ian Fleming. He is a Royal Navy lieutenant commander and the aid to Admiral Godfrey, the director of Naval Intelligence. Fleming was involved with Stephenson and with Donovan back in '41. After a recent trip to America with Godfrey, he asked his boss and Stephenson if he could observe training here. He has inserted himself in several exercises. The camp supervisor hates the idea, as does our chief of training, Bill Brocker. But the Admiral, Mr. Stephenson and Brigadier Gubbins wanted it to happen, so we have been saddled with this visitor ever since. His brother, Peter, was with the SOE at the beginning, though he's shifted to some other secret outfit."

"Where is Fleming now?"

Creed pointed to another man preparing to enter the shooting house. "That's Fleming. Number 001 on his boiler suit. Quite a good shot with the Browning. He is about to go through the course with the revolver right now."

Lundin watched as the instructor gave Fleming some last-minute instructions. Lundin turned to Creed and said, "I'm going to go talk to Jovanovic. When Fleming comes out of the building, please bring him over to me."

Creed nodded. "Happy to do so, Miles."

Lundin walked over to the seating area. Jovanovic was sitting next to the ATA female, the two engaged in conversation. He watched their body language and wondered if Jovanovic might have a crush on the pilot. Could that be a motive? After all, Jovanovic might have known Novak from the Navy. And, he wondered if Jovanovic and Novak knew each other from before. Novak was from St. Catherines. Where did Jovanovic hail from and, for that matter, what sort of family name was Jovanovic?

Lundin decided it was too early to ask those sorts of questions. First, he needed to get the emigre comfortable with questioning.

After that he could take the questioning in any direction he chose. He decided to keep the initial discussion polite and even friendly. While sometimes it was useful to play the role of the stern Mountie, he found that it didn't hurt to try the friendly Mountie persona first. Especially when you were working with emigres whose experience with European law enforcement was less kind. After all, the stern or even angry Mountie was an easy shift if Jovanovic started to lie to him. As he approached, Lundin overheard their conversation.

Thomas whispered, "I think that Mountie looks quite smart in his Stetson hat."

Jovanovic countered, "I think the Mountie looks terrifying. As a child in Belgrade, my life was filled with men in uniform using their authorities to take whatever they pleased and punishing anyone who got in the way. I grew up with a healthy fear of anyone in uniform. My parents were horrified the day I returned home after basic training in a Canadian Navy uniform. They saw my new status as a sign that I had chosen a dark path. I knew differently: If Canada was at war, I wanted to help."

Thomas touched Jovanovic's shoulder. "Petyr, the only thing you should fear now are the Nazis."

Lundin decided at that point to interrupt. "Petyr Jovanovic?"

The voice seemed far less threatening than Jovanovic expected. He stood at attention and said, "Machinist mate third class Jovanovic, sir."

Lundin did his best not to laugh. For the first time that day, he finally had someone willing to accept his authority. Still, he didn't want this interview to end up with "yes sir, no sir" responses. He said in his most gentle voice, "Jovanovic, please stand at ease. I just need to ask a few questions."

Thomas interjected, "And your name, Sergeant?"

Lundin thought the former pilot's voice sounded quite pleasant even if he didn't like the fact that she had interrupted. He gave her a stern look and said, "Senior Staff Sergeant Lundin, Royal Canadian Mounted Police."

Thomas didn't even try to stifle a giggle. She said, "We already knew you were with the Force. I mean really, who else wears that uniform and a Stetson? I suspect you could walk into a bar anywhere in the world and people would know you are a Mountie." She paused to watch as Lundin began to blush. "We are absolutely at your service, Senior Staff Sergeant. How can we help?"

Lundin could see the pilot was playing with him and that made him both frustrated and confused. Lundin had been a single man for a long time, and he had lost the ability or the willingness to flirt. He needed to talk to Jovanovic without the intrusion of this … pilot. He said, "Ma'am, were you part of the kayak exercise on the twelfth?"

"Nope. They had me working on agent communications. Classroom stuff."

Lundin nodded. "Then, I am interested only in your colleague. But what is your name?"

Thomas stood up and held out her hand. "Flight Lieutenant Beatrice Thomas, Air Transport Auxiliary, though I suspect shortly I will be just Thomas, a Canadian in the SOE." Lundin took her hand and found a surprisingly firm handshake. She continued to look directly into his eyes. "Just let me know if I can help."

Lundin continued to blush. "Thanks, Flight Lieutenant. I need to talk in private to Machinist Mate Jovanovic, so if you would excuse us?" He raised the open palm of his left hand and pointed away from the bench. Jovanovic followed.

Lundin started to ask questions as soon as they were out of earshot from Thomas. "Can you tell me what you know about the man who you pulled out of the lake?"

"Sir, I know nothing about him. Honestly, I didn't see him in the water. That was Commander Fleming who saw him floating nearby. I was paddling the kayak and the commander was steering. It was very dark. I suppose the commander was looking around for obstacles and for our landing site when he saw the man."

"Did you recognize him?"

"He was face down in the water. The commander dragged him close to the kayak and then we pulled him to the beach. He remained face down as the commander pulled him up on the beach. After that,

Captain Creed told me to go to a waiting jeep. I did that, and have tried ever since to focus on training." He looked up at the Mountie and said, "Sir, did he die in training? We do many dangerous things here. Was it a kayak accident?"

Lundin thought for a moment. Jovanovic sounded both sincere and confused. And, he asked a question that anyone who didn't know about the murder would ask. Specifically, he asked how did the man die? Often that was one of the first clues in a murder investigation. While many might know about a death nearby, very few expect the reason is murder. After all, whether in industry, farming, mining or now the military, life in Canada was dangerous and accidents happened all the time. Here was a man who assumed immediately that it was an accident. Either he was truly surprised by the events or an exceptional actor. Lundin thought Jovanovic was hardly capable of acting, especially since English wasn't his native tongue. "Where are you from, Jovanovic?"

"Hamilton, Ontario, sir."

"I understand you served in the Navy. Were you in the fleet?"

"Yes, sir. I served on convoy duty in a destroyer escort, the Fraser."

"Why volunteer for this duty if you already were serving Canada?"

"There was a call for individuals who spoke Serbo-Croatian. I was born in Belgrade and emigrated when my parents left Yugoslavia in 1932. I assumed if Canada needed my language skills, it was my duty to volunteer."

"Dangerous duty, Jovanovic."

Jovanovic smiled for the first time. "Sir, you must understand I was in an old destroyer, serving below decks on twelve-hour shifts, waiting for a German torpedo to sink my ship with me trapped inside. I think that was far more dangerous than what they expect me to do here."

"Fair point. Have you ever met a man named Novak?"

Jovanovic shrugged. "There are multiple families named Novak in Hamilton. It is a very common Yugoslavian name. Why?"

"The man you dragged out of Lake Ontario was named Novak. Ned Novak."

"Is he from Hamilton? How did his body end up near the camp?"

Lundin had watched Jovanovic's responses. He did not seem to understand that Novak was a resident of the camp or that this was a murder investigation. Rather than waste his time, he decided to end the conversation. "We are still trying to understand any of it, Machinist Mate Jovanovic. I will be talking to Commander Fleming next. If you remember anything later, I will be staying at the camp for at least one more day. You can contact me through Captain Creed."

Jovanovic came to the position of attention and rendered a smart salute. Lundin returned the salute. He said, "One last question. What were you talking about with the flight lieutenant?"

This time it was Jovanovic who blushed. "I know we are not supposed to ask about the past. I just wondered how she became a pilot. She is a very capable woman."

"What did she say?"

"She joked and said it was a long story, and one that she couldn't tell. She is very nice."

Lundin wasn't surprised that Jovanovic was interested in Thomas. He suspected she had that effect on most of her colleagues. He said, "Off you go then. Back to training."

He watched as the Serb jogged back to the firearms building. Jovanovic was certainly strong enough to break a man's neck, and he was receiving training to do so. There just didn't seem to be any motive or, for that matter, opportunity given the rigorous training program. Perhaps not exactly a dead end, but certainly not a likely suspect.

As he walked back to the firearms building, he saw Creed approach with Fleming in tow. The man in the green jumpsuit did not walk like any Navy officer Lundin had ever met. Like Creed, he walked like an athlete. Unlike Creed, he walked with the insouciance of a young fop walking to some nightclub. Lundin wondered how in the world this man ever reached the rank of lieutenant commander; perhaps the Englishman had family connections that had purchased his commission? His brown hair was cut in a civilian rather than military style. Even in a jumpsuit he seemed exceptionally confident, perhaps over-confident.

Creed spoke first. "Miles, here's Commander Fleming."

Before Lundin could respond, Fleming held out his hand and said, "Fleming, Ian Fleming. Please call me Ian, and I hope I can call you Miles."

Lundin took Fleming's hand. While he had expected a relatively soft grip, instead Fleming's handshake was dry, strong and vigorous. "A pleasure." Lundin turned to Creed and said, "I would like to talk to Commander Fleming on my own. We'll just take a walk toward the beach." Creed nodded and walked over to the bench where Thomas and Jovanovic were seated.

Fleming was the first to speak. "They don't like me here, you know. They think I am some toff from London who is on a holiday in Canada. Plus, they don't much like Navy men here, not that I'm much of a Navy man."

Lundin decided that if Fleming wanted to talk, he would let him. "Why are you here?"

"You see, the admiral believes there is a need for an independent company of commandos under his jurisdiction for intelligence collection operations. There are many intelligence gaps in our knowledge of German technology, especially German torpedoes and German radars. There is no one in the intelligence services capable of conducting both commando operations and intelligence collection. Our commando training is designed to create raiders who can kill and destroy. What we need are raiders able to steal items and disappear. They should only kill if they must do so. A different sort of commando."

Lundin interjected, "The admiral?"

"Oh, sorry. I am the personal assistant to the Director of Naval Intelligence, Rear Admiral John Godfrey. He periodically tasks me to sort out specific challenges that no one else seems to have the imagination to solve. That's the Navy for you, I suppose." Fleming paused for a moment, expecting Lundin to ask another question. When he didn't, Fleming continued, "So, back to our problem. We need to steal German kit, return it to Britain and hand it over to the boffins at the Admiralty. The SOE program seemed closer to our needs for training our pirates. I was in North America with the admiral, and when I heard of this course I asked if I could attend. He engaged M and with both of their permissions, here I am."

"M?"

"Colonel Gubbins. He is the chief of operations for the SOE. He signs his message traffic with the letter M. I suspect he will be the head of SOE before too long. He is an expert in irregular warfare, faced it in Ireland and Norway and even wrote a book on the subject. Quite the Renaissance man."

"So, you are here to observe the training and determine if it might match your needs at the Admiralty?"

"Exactly so. Of course, that doesn't mean the instructors have to like me or even treat me as a fellow officer. I am, after all, a *reserve officer.*" Fleming reached into the pocket of his jumpsuit and pulled out a silver cigarette case. Popping it open, he offered one to Lundin and took one for himself. He then returned the cigarette case and pulled out a silver lighter, lighting their cigarettes. Lundin didn't smoke, but early on learned if you were offered something you took it. Even as a non-smoker, he could tell that these cigarettes were custom made. And he suspected Fleming's lighter would cost nearly his full month's RCMP salary. Fleming seemed something of a dandy.

Before Lundin could form any additional thoughts on the matter, Fleming continued, "It doesn't help that my brother was an SOE officer who left them to work with the propaganda people, the Political Warfare Executive. So, I'm not only a useless visitor but from an untrustworthy family." As he expelled smoke from both nostrils, Fleming continued, "Miles, I would be willing to bet they see you in the same vein."

Lundin was used to his role as an outsider, but he had to laugh at Fleming's remark. "Commander, I think you have quite the skill as an observer."

"I've always been a bit of an outsider. Social survival in England means observing people and noting their strengths and weaknesses. Since we are both outsiders, why don't we at least collaborate? You want to know about the night I pulled the body out of Lake Ontario, and I want to know why so many of these instructors are so tight-lipped about the event."

Lundin smiled. "You first."

Fleming seemed to enjoy the banter and responded with enthusiasm. "The training exercise was simple enough. We were driven to a dock about thirty miles west of here. They took us out to an old rust bucket they called a mother ship. We launched from that ship. Six men in three boats. They are called folboats because they are collapsible kayaks made of waterproof canvas with folding wooden frames. The Commandos have been using them since the beginning of the war. We launched just after sunset. The training mission was to head southeast back toward camp and to take photos of a General Motors factory near Oshawa on the lake that makes aircraft parts — or at least that's what they said in the mission brief. We were issued waterproof cameras, binoculars and waterproof notepads. It was a classic recce mission. Get close to the target, observe as much as possible without being seen and then get back to base."

"Were you in sight of the other two boats the entire time?"

"More or less. There was good moonlight so you could see the shore, and the other boats were silhouetted by the shoreline. We were moving in line with Petyr and I in the last boat."

Lundin thought for a moment. If nothing else, the case might help the Force improve Canadian industrial security. He said, "Any sign of patrol boats?"

"Oh, they were out and probably looking for us. But the folboat has a very low profile above the water. In the dark, you would never see us. Even if you used a spotlight, I think you might miss us unless the light glinted off the binoculars or the camera lenses."

Fleming took another long drag from his cigarette and smiled. "Look, you really don't have to finish the gasper if it's not to your taste. However, it is sufficiently rare in Canada that I would like to keep it if you don't mind."

Lundin dutifully handed back the smoldering but unsmoked cigarette and watched as Fleming knocked the embers off and placed it behind his left ear. Once again, Lundin realized that this was a man who observed even the most minute details. That could be very helpful or very dangerous depending on which side he was on. Lundin decided to see just how observant Fleming was. "What did you first notice about the body?"

"Clearly, he had a broken neck." Fleming shook his head. "One of the techniques taught here is how to break a sentry's neck. The body was a victim of that technique."

"So, he didn't drown?"

"Is that what they told you? What rubbish! They all know better and should know that you would find out sooner or later. Oh … you already knew, eh?"

Lundin nodded. "It is my job."

"Well good on you making sure who you can and can't trust here. I haven't figured that out yet and I've been here almost three weeks. I can tell you that Petyr is a good chap. Keeps to himself and seems a classic man of the soil." Fleming paused for a moment and said, "I say, are you staying overnight?"

"I'm staying until I solve this case."

Fleming looked at his stainless-steel waterproof Rolex watch. "My training exercises end tonight just after 1800hrs. Any chance you might want to take me into Oshawa? There is a hotel there that pours a decent bourbon whiskey."

"You aren't bound to the camp?"

"Remember, I'm an outsider and that means I don't have to follow all the camp rules." He looked up at Lundin. "Oh dear, I don't suppose you are teetotal?"

Lundin laughed for the first time that day. "No, Commander. I am not teetotal, and I think a whiskey might be a good idea. Can I get a room there?"

"Indeed. It's called the Hotel Genosha. Clean, reliable and a couple of different restaurants. And the bartender at Harry's Hideaway knows his business. I have used their rooms more than once. Nothing like Toronto, but I suspect a Mountie is used to far worse."

"Where do we meet?"

"This isn't some secret rendezvous. The staff will be happy to see me leave. Just meet me in front of the headquarters building at 1800hrs and we'll be away from the controls of the camp cadre." With that and making no other apologies for his departure, Fleming turned and headed back to training at a jog.

Lundin shook his head and walked slowly back. Creed was waiting for him by the benches. Both Jovanovic and Thomas were gone. Creed raised an eyebrow. "Productive?"

"He's an odd chap, but seems friendly enough. We are going for a drink later. Want to join us?"

"Oh my, Miles. You haven't quite grasped the camp lifestyle. I have a night training exercise that starts in an hour and will run through midnight. No drinks for me." As they walked to the jeep, he said, "We should be able to catch up with Ken Stevens now." They jumped in and drove toward an odd-shaped building that seemed to stand in front of a fence of antennas.

CHAPTER SIX —
A VISIT TO HYDRA

They pulled up to the front door of the building that served as the home of HYDRA, a rectangular clapboard structure with small windows just under the roofline on all four sides. Otherwise, the only break in the structure was a metal double door big enough for a jeep or a small truck to drive through. Two guards in Canadian military police uniform were posted at the door. As Creed and Lundin walked up, they first came to the position of attention and then at port arms, with their rifles and bayonets covering the entrance.

Creed said, "We are here to meet with Mr. Stevens. Please let him know we are waiting outside."

One of the MPs said, "Sir, please state your name and rank."

Creed looked at Lundin and said, "It's a little different for HYDRA." He turned to the MP and said, "Captain Hamish Creed, tradecraft instructor here at STS 103. This is Senior Staff Sergeant Miles Lundin of the Royal Canadian Mounted Police. We are here to speak about the death of Mr. Edward Novak, who was one of Mr. Stevens' team leaders."

The MP nodded. He turned to his colleague, whispered something to him and then entered the metal door. Lundin took the time to observe the building and the guard mount. They had parked near a covered 2 ½ ton Chevrolet cargo truck with a canvas top. The guards were disciplined, and their uniforms were well-cared for but not new. These were military policemen who had been in service for some time. The guards at the door were both sergeants. Lundin looked for and eventually spotted two pairs of guards walking the perimeter in opposite directions near the antenna field. Assuming the guard mount was four-six hours long, that meant a full platoon of Canadian Army military policemen were assigned to protect the facility. It might not mean much in a compound full of student commandos, but it would certainly deter adolescents from the nearby farms from curious visits to HYDRA. It also meant it was unlikely that the murder occurred in or near this building — unless an entire guard mount was part of a conspiracy. Lundin noted that he would need to speak to the platoon commander or, better still, the senior sergeant about the guard rotations.

Ken Stevens walked out from the metal doors and greeted them. He was a small man, balding and about 20 pounds overweight. Unlike everyone Lundin had met so far, he was dressed like a man who had just left an office in Toronto. He wore wool trousers held up with fabric braces, a white shirt with sleeves rolled up to the elbows and a polka-dot bow tie. He was wearing brown brogue shoes and a small dress watch on a brown strap. When he spoke, the voice was very low pitch and corresponding volume. "Gentlemen, I hope you understand I can't invite you in."

Lundin nodded. For the first time that day he had his notebook out and a pencil in hand. Finally, he would be able to gather some details about Novak. He decided to keep up the fiction that Novak drowned. "I don't need to see inside your building unless you have a large pool that could be used to drown a man."

Stevens shook his head. "No, just racks of electronics and tables for the monitors who send and receive messages. We have a telex section and a radio section. Ned was the night supervisor for both sections."

Lundin knew he needed to get Stevens to walk away from the building, if for no other reason than to prevent the military policemen from overhearing his set of questions. As with Jovanovic, he simply raised his left arm and used his open hand to point toward the truck and the gravel road leading back to the rest of the camp. "I hope you don't mind taking a little walk?"

"Not at all. I get very little opportunity for fresh air." Stevens walked with Lundin and Creed down the driveway, their shoes crunching on the gravel. Lundin considered how far he wanted Stevens to walk. The man did not look like the picture of health.

He stopped and said, "Mr. Stevens, I need to ask a few questions about Mr. Novak. I'm going to start with Novak's schedule. When did you know he was missing?"

Even in the perfect 60-degree fall afternoon, Stevens was already sweating when he turned to Lundin. "Ned was supposed to pick up the night shift at 1800hrs. He no longer had a specific workstation. Rather, as shift supervisor he simply wandered between the radio and the telex sections making sure everything was running smoothly. I looked at the shift log for that night. He signed in with the MPs at 1750hrs. Now, we don't keep track of individuals who leave the building for short periods of time. After all, they need to use the out-houses and they need a periodic break in the fresh air to keep sharp. So, no one seemed to notice he was gone until Captain Marks woke me up at midnight to say that they found Ned's body in the lake."

"Captain Marks?"

"He's the platoon commander for the Canadian Army MPs who guard HYDRA. He first called Mr. Hardcastle, the HYDRA commander, and then called me."

Creed interjected, "William Hardcastle is the HYDRA lead. His quarters are next to mine and we play a bit of chess together. I made sure he was informed as soon as we realized it was Novak."

Lundin nodded. He really didn't want or need Creed's help, but he didn't know how to separate him from the discussion. He thought for a minute and said, "Hamish, can you ask the MPs if they can contact their commander? I would like to arrange an interview with him or with their platoon sergeant sometime tomorrow. I honestly don't care when tomorrow. Simply at his convenience."

He turned to Stevens and said, "Mr. Stevens, I will need to talk to you again. I realize you are currently working the night shift at HYDRA. Can we arrange some time tomorrow just before you start your shift? Perhaps at 1500hrs? I need to know more about Novak and you seem to be the only person who can give me a better understanding of the man."

Lundin noted Stevens looked uncomfortable about the request. He seemed torn between rejecting it out of hand and accepting the logic. There was a long pause before Stevens finally answered, "I suppose tomorrow at 1500hrs would be fine. I'm not sure how I can help, but I will do my best."

"Thank you. And thank you for taking the time out from what is clearly an important job." Lundin offered his hand and received a sweaty and limp handshake in return. Stevens turned on his heel and walked quickly back to the HYDRA building. He passed Creed.

"Odd duck, eh?" Creed winked as he said it.

"I reckon he is more comfortable with wires and tubes and antennas than with people. Still, if anyone is going to give me an understanding of Novak as a member of HYDRA, it is going to be Stevens. Does he live in quarters here on-post or is he off-post?"

"Nearly everyone lives on-post. Only a few of the local support staff, cleaners and such, come in from Oshawa."

"Before we call it a day, can you take me to Novak's quarters? That will capture much of what I need to accomplish in my initial investigation."

"How about I take you back to your vehicle and then you follow me to the residential area? I will need to leave you there and return to my duties for the night training exercise."

"Hamish, you have been very generous with your time. Do you have keys to Novak's quarters?"

Creed smiled and held up a small key ring with two keys. "Already ahead of you. And, the MPs thought the best time to see their platoon sergeant would be the afternoon shift change at 1500hrs."

CHAPTER SEVEN —
ROOM 12 AND THE REMAINS OF A MAN

nside the building where Edward Novak had lived, Lundin found himself thinking back to the housing where he had begun his own training for the Great War more than 20 years ago. Like the rest of Camp X, the residential area had a military feel. The buildings were two-story structures, with entrances and stairwells at both ends. There was a coal-fired boiler furnace at one end of the building, with heating ducts running in the floors. Bathrooms and shower facilities were located at both ends of the long hallways. There were ten rooms on each side of the central hallway. The walls were thin and the heating would be minimal in the rooms at the end opposite the furnace. It reminded Lundin of barracks life when he was training for the Royal Rifles. He walked to room 12 on the first floor, used the keys provided by Creed and let himself in.

The room was small, ten by ten feet, with a single bed, a washstand, a desk and chair and an armoire. Lundin looked around the spartan quarters and said to himself, "Well, it probably seemed spacious to a man who came from quarters on a ship." The room was clean and tidy. The bed was made to a military standard, with tight-fitting sheets and squared corners of a single, brown wool blanket. The desk had a small stack of writing paper next to the blotter. An electric lamp was squared off with some precision in the corner of the desk. There was a fountain pen at the top of the blotter and an ink bottle directly above it. It could easily have been set out for a military or RCMP inspection.

Lundin was never comfortable digging through the lives of victims. He felt that dead men had as much right to privacy as the living. He seldom had to search through former possessions in previous murder investigations. The cases that the Force took on rarely evolved like a "who done it" mystery novel. A rural crime usually meant the entire community knew precisely both the victim and the likely villain. Often, the only challenge was to find proof or to persuade the villain to confess. For that reason, he rarely had to dig into the remnants of the victim's life. All he had to do was ask the neighbors. This was a different sort of case, and that meant Novak's privacy could not be considered.

Lundin checked the desk drawer. A half dozen white envelopes, a roll of stamps and a Bible, in both Cyrillic and English script. During his first weeks in the Toronto barracks, Lundin had conducted multiple investigations in the Yugoslavian community, so he wasn't surprised that Novak was devout or that he would be reading his Bible in Serbian. He also knew that several religious organizations, including Catholic orders, offered a Bible in English and Serbian as a means of teaching English to new emigres. Lundin flipped through the Bible to see if Novak had a favorite passage or a scrap of paper used as a bookmark. He remembered his grandmother was always using whatever was at hand — shopping lists, bills, postcards — as her Bible bookmarks. She regularly forgot where they were and Lundin had been sent around the house to find them. The Bible was always his first stop.

He found the bookmark in the Old Testament, chapter 32 of Deuteronomy. Lundin read the chapter, which he knew from Sunday school as the Song of Moses. It was verse 35 that caught his attention:

It is mine to avenge; I will repay. In due time their foot will slip; their day of disaster is near and their doom rushes upon them.

Lundin sat down on the wooden chair and reread the entire chapter twice. What might this mean? On the wider scale, this could easily be a verse used by the oppressed against the oppressor. Yugoslavia was occupied by the Nazis, and there was a Yugoslavian resistance. This might simply be Novak taking solace in the fact that there would be a victory in time.

But, what if this was more about his local life here at Camp X? Here was a man who was murdered and thrown into Lake Ontario, most probably because his murderer thought his body would be washed away, never to be found. Vengeance? For the first time in the investigation, Lundin began to wonder about Novak the man rather than Novak as simply a body on the shoreline. The Bible and the Bible verse hinted that Novak's possessions just might give him some insight into the reason for the murder and, with some luck, the murderer.

He opened the armoire. There were a series of shirts and trousers neatly hung with shirts to the left, trousers to the right. Novak was a man of simple style: four white cotton dress shirts; two heavier wool shirts in navy blue; three sets of trousers, all dark grey wool. Next to them hung one set of dungarees, likely Canadian Navy issue. In the very far right of the armoire were two Canadian Navy uniforms. Both were dark blue, with his radioman rank stitched on the left sleeve. His Navy cap hung from one of the hangers. Stitched on the cap in gold braid was HMCS Assiniboine. Lundin took down the name of the ship for further research. At the very least, he now knew where Novak served before coming to HYDRA. The uniforms suggested Lundin was still in the Navy. Did he return to civilian life or was he attached to HYDRA after serving at sea? More questions floated into Lundin's mind.

A classic sea chest was below the clothes. It was a wood-and-leather affair that covered the entire bottom of the armoire. Lundin pulled it out and turned it so he could open the chest without obstruction from the bed, desk, chair or armoire. He looked for something to place it on so that he wouldn't have to move to his knees. His hopes dashed, Lundin lowered himself down on the quilted rug that lay between the bed and the door. It was not the most comfortable of positions, but it seemed the only way to take his time with the chest. Just before he opened the lid, he noticed that there were scuff marks on the plank floor suggesting that this was precisely the way the owner accessed his goods.

Inside the chest, he found a wooden shelf with neatly folded underwear and socks. Just as Novak's outer clothing was simple, so his undergarments were as well: five sets of white t-shirts; five sets of white boxer shorts; five sets of white wool socks. While this offered little revelation as to Novak's character, it did remind Lundin to ask what Novak was wearing when he was pulled out of the water. Given Fleming's apparent observation skills, Lundin took another note to ask. He pulled the wooden shelf up and out of the chest and set it to his right. Below the shelf were a pair of Navy-issued work boots, a pair of rope-soled canvas shoes and a heavy, Navy-issued wool sweater. The boots were polished and slightly tacky from some sort of waterproofing; the canvas shoes were clean. The wool sweater had a light smell of naphtha to keep moths from eating away at the fabric. Lundin pulled the shoes and the sweater out of the trunk and set them next to his left hip.

Below these items was a plywood section with two round holes designed to allow the owner to pull up the plywood to access the final layer. Lundin pulled up the section and set it aside on top of the sweater and the shoes. This revealed what could only be called a small cabinet of curiosities.

On the left side of the trunk was an aluminum hinged box no more than three inches deep that ran the length of the box. On the lid was imprinted **NOVAK, Edward Anton, A22124, HMS Campbeltown.** Lundin puzzled over the identification of a different ship, and this time from the Royal Navy. This generated another notation in his notebook.

He opened the lid to find Novak's identity disks, his enlistment papers, a Canadian Navy-issued pocketknife and three medals. The first was easy to identify since it was a star-shaped medal embossed with words, The Atlantic Star. Lundin knew from previous investigations that this was the standard service medal issued to sailors involved in convoy duty. The second medal was equally easy to identify. The front had an image of the King and the reverse was embossed, "For Good Conduct." The third medal was a puzzle. It was a standard Canadian Volunteer Service Medal, but the clasp above the medal read St. Nazaire. Another piece of the puzzle went into Lundin's notebook.

To the right of the aluminum case were a series of letters between Novak and a Miroslav Novosel. The letters dated from May 1942, with the last one from Novosel having arrived just a week before Novak's death. Novosel's address was a collective military address in Scotland. Lundin knew this was common for soldiers assigned to remote military camps or military training. Novosel's rank was listed as sergeant. When Lundin started to open the letters, he realized that they were in Serbo-Croatian. Both Novak and Novosel used the Romanized alphabet, but that hardly helped. As he opened the most recent letter from Novosel, a small black and white photo fell into the chest. Lundin could see it was a picture of a half-dozen men in combat gear taken on some mountainside. As he reached for the photo, everything went black.

CHAPTER EIGHT — THE BEGINNING OF A PARTNERSHIP?

Lundin woke with a wet washcloth over his face. He was lying in bed, and someone was talking. It took some concentration to get the words to make any sense. Finally, he heard a voice say, "Well, are you going to open your eyes or do I call the coroner?"

He pulled the washcloth off his face. His eyes took some time to focus. He was still in Novak's room, which was lighted in a yellow glow from the single desk lamp. He said, "How long?"

Fleming looked at him and said, "About a half hour since I arrived. I have no idea how long before that. By the way, Miles: Do you know you are one heavy load?"

Lundin slowly raised his left hand to his eyes and focused on his watch. It was 1900hrs. "Damnation! It was about 1730hrs when I got here. I have never been knocked out that long in my entire time as a Mountie."

"Well, you have never been attacked by folks who are trained to kill or disable silently, leaving no marks. That's one of the best things they teach here."

Lundin's voice was a croak. "So, we can probably eliminate all the radio boffins from the equation."

"I would say so. Hmmm, would you like a little tipple to smooth the rough edges?" Fleming offered a silver hip flask wrapped in doeskin leather. Miles sat up. A wave of nausea rushed through him as he took the flask. He swallowed a bit of whiskey and had to admit, it did make him feel better. His eyes began to focus. Fleming was in a tan, roll-neck sweater, navy-blue wool trousers and the same boots he wore earlier in the day. Behind him was a leather pilot's jacket hung on the door of the armoire.

"Not to worry, Miles. I'm not going to say anything to anyone about this misadventure. Only you, your assailant and yours truly know they got the drop on you."

"Somehow that doesn't make me feel any better."

"Will you feel better to know they didn't take your service revolver?"

Lundin suddenly realized that his Sam Brown belt and his tunic were hanging on a coat hanger in the armoire. He said, "Was I just slumped over the sea chest when you found me?"

"Sea chest? What sea chest?"

"Oh, that's just grand. A sea chest was in the bottom of the armoire. I was looking through it when I was hit." He reached up and started tentatively to feel the back of his head. He couldn't feel any bruising.

Fleming said, "I don't think you were hit. They teach a strangulation hold here that only takes about ten seconds to work. Blocks the arteries and windpipe. And, it would appear, it also blocks your memory of the event. They say anyone can take on anyone, regardless of size. It would appear the instructor cadre aren't lying, since there is no one in the student body or the instructor cadre your size." Fleming recovered his flask and took a swig. "Now tell me about the sea chest."

"It was in the bottom on the armoire. I opened it and found a basic sailor kit including underwear, boots and a sweater. Below that I found a shelf with an aluminum tin with Novak's medals. And there were letters in Serbian and a photo of what looked like a commando team. The tin listed Novak as a seaman on the HMS Campbeltown. What is a Canadian doing on a Royal Navy ship?"

"A better question might be, how in the world did Novak survive the Campbeltown?"

"Eh?"

"I suppose the operation is still classified so it hasn't made the papers yet. It was a destroyer used on a raid in St. Nazaire, France."

"Novak had a medal with a clasp that said St. Nazaire."

"Well, it's a good long story. Do you think you can get up so we can go into town and get some dinner and more whiskey? I promise to continue once we are out of a dead man's room."

Lundin sat up slowly, put his feet on the floor and tested his balance. Once he was certain that he could stand up, he walked over to the armoire and pulled on his tunic and Sam Brown belt. As he did so, he looked in the armoire. Absolutely nothing was different from the earlier search. Except, of course, the sea chest was gone. He shook his head and said, "Well, that was a rookie mistake."

"Don't beat yourself up. This place is supposed to be one of the most secure in Canada. How could you have expected to be attacked?"

Lundin put on his Stetson, closed the armoire door and said, "That's probably what Novak thought as well."

As Fleming walked to the door he turned and said, "Fair point."

CHAPTER NINE — AN ADVENTURE STORY

Lundin allowed Fleming to drive them both to Oshawa. While he was recovering quickly, he didn't want to trust his reflexes on a night drive on a rural road. Fleming was a competent driver who liked to use the shift on the column more than Lundin would approve. In the yellow light of the Buick's speedometer dial and the four subdials, he noticed Fleming's face took on a hawk-like impression with his hooked nose and sunken cheeks. They arrived at the hotel in one piece, which was all that Lundin could have hoped for given Fleming's passion for speed and speed-shifting around the narrow roads leading to the city.

Lundin had to admit that he felt much better after a restaurant meal. He ate baked haddock with chips and a Molson's ale. Fleming had steak and chips with a large bourbon whiskey. As an English gent, he had expected Fleming was a gin or Scotch whisky drinker. Bourbon was a very American whiskey. Most Canadians drank rye, especially Canadian Club. When he asked, Fleming waved his cigarette toward the drink and said, "I picked up the taste on a previous trip to the States. And, it is said that it is the healthiest of the whiskies." He laughed. "I am very focused on my health."

Over dinner, they had talked more on whiskey and on Canada and Lundin's time in the Northwest Territories. Lundin told a story about running a dog team between villages around Great Bear and Great Slave lakes. Fleming was a good listener, and as the meal ended he said, "Miles, you have had more than your share of adventures. I am just starting my life and I suspect my adventures will be far less dangerous."

"Unless, of course, we get close to our murderer."

"I fully intend for you to get close while I am in the rear. It will be up to you when it comes to the arrest."

"If you are going to stick with me until the end, I can't promise that you won't be in the line of fire. It is just that way sometimes."

Fleming raised his nearly empty glass in a toast. "Well, I do have my own weapons, so I will do my best to hold up my end of the bargain."

They were drinking coffee when they finally returned to discussing the case. The restaurant was empty, which meant they were left alone except for the occasional visit by a waitress to fill their coffee cups and to refresh Fleming's whiskey. The waitress also ran the front desk of the hotel, and had given them the keys to their rooms. She was friendly but seemed to know when guests wanted to be left alone. After she cleared the plates, she did just that.

Fleming began, "So, let me tell you an adventure story to explain the St. Nazaire operation. It is about the German pocket battleships and their fast cruisers. While everyone is worried about the German U-boats, as well they should be, these German surface warships are dangerous to both convoys and our fleet. After we had some luck sinking the Bismarck, we needed to make the rest of their battlefleet as uncomfortable as possible. We did that in Jutland in the Great War, but now the German warships are out in the Atlantic. Well, no matter how well you build a ship, it must come in for service at some point and, ideally, servicing means time at a dry dock." He took a sip of his whiskey. "Following me so far?"

"Ian, I'm following, but I don't know where we are going. How about getting to the point?"

Fleming laughed. "You aren't the first man to say my tales are too long and too complicated. Still, if you want to understand why we raided the St. Nazaire dry docks, you need to know why they were important. They were important because they were the only dry docks on the Atlantic coast that could service these German warships."

"Hence, the raid you were talking about."

Fleming raised his glass in another salute. "Exactly. First, we asked the Royal Air Force to do the job. I'm not sure if it is simply a function of their skills, the complicated nature of the docks or their disinterest in assisting the Navy, but they couldn't do it. So, that meant it was a job for the Combined Operations lot."

"Combined Operations?"

"It is simply the official term for the partnership between the Commandos, the Royal Navy and, less often, the Royal Air Force. All under the command of Mountbatten."

"As in Vice Admiral Louis Mountbatten?"

"Indeed. The outfit is called combined operations because the Commandos always make their assault from the sea, and that means the Royal Navy must deliver them and bring them home after they have done their raid. In the case of St. Nazaire, the Royal Navy did far more than the delivery."

"Enter the Campbeltown?"

"Exactly. The Campbeltown was an old American destroyer that was no longer up to convoy duty. She was old but she was seaworthy, just the ship for the mission."

"For the raid?"

"Not exactly a raid, Miles. We used the entire ship as a very large, very well-placed bomb."

Fleming waved to the waitress and she delivered another glass of bourbon. Lundin was amazed at Fleming's capacity for drink with no sign of any effect on his mind. He wondered if, once they stood up, Fleming would be in any shape to make it to the rooms they had rented for the night. His musings were cut short by Fleming's story.

"So, the plan was relatively simple. Attack the entire port of St. Nazaire at once. There was the dry dock, a half-dozen submarine pens and fuel storage. Given the size of the facility, it was also a German Navy headquarters. The Combined Operations boffins filled the bow of the Campbeltown with explosives with a set of time fuses. The attack on the dry dock involved ramming the gates, scuttling the Campbeltown and then detonating the explosives to fracture the concrete dock itself. Meanwhile, commandos delivered by the destroyer and escort vessels attacked the remaining facilities."

"Successful?"

"Oh, dear, yes! At great cost. The Campbeltown came under enormous fire as she approached the docks, as did the escort vessels. And while the other raid targets were all hit, nearly the entire No. 2 Commando force was either killed or captured. Most of the Campbeltown skeleton crew were recovered by an escort vessel. Several of the ship's officers remained at the docks to ensure the explosives did their job."

"So, Novak must have been…?"

"Well, as a radioman he would have been crucial to the operation because they had to keep the entire force together, initially using signal lanterns. Once they were engaged in the fight, he would be using radio traffic to manage the multiple pieces of the operation. He would have been in the middle of the most difficult Navy communications mission so far in this war."

"And why would he have ended up at HYDRA?"

Fleming had just finished his third bourbon. He raised an eyebrow. "Who knows? Perhaps he was wounded or suffered from shell shock; perhaps the fleet decided that Novak was just the man to keep tabs on the development of a secret communications facility. I have no insight into this. HYDRA is a hush-hush facility. When the admiral toured the camp only he was allowed into the building, along with the HYDRA commander. The post commander wasn't even let inside."

Lundin was drinking coffee at about the same pace as Fleming was drinking bourbon and smoking his special-batch cigarettes. His mind was racing with the events of his first day on the investigation. By early morning he would have to give a report to the chief inspector and, so far, he had more questions than answers. He said, "Is any of this likely to have a role in Novak's death?"

Fleming shook his head. "Miles, based on what you saw in the sea chest and the fact that it's no longer in our possession, it seems hard to imagine that it doesn't play a role. This sounds more and more like an espionage case to me."

Lundin thought for a moment. He was bothered with Fleming

assuming a role in the investigation. Still, the English dandy had access to a world that was currently outside Lundin's experience. And so far, he was the only one at the camp who wasn't either lying outright or choosing to be very careful with the truth. Lundin had not considered Novak as a target in some Nazi plot, so he used an open-ended question to get Fleming to continue his line of thought. "Espionage? How is that possible?"

"Miles, think about the larger context. We have a man who had access to secret communications and secret codes. Based on your description from the sea chest, he also had a background in commando operations and ..." Fleming paused to stub out his cigarette, "he was in written communication with another Yugoslav who is either training to be a commando or is already one stationed in Scotland. There are plenty of reasons for a Nazi, some Irish Sinn Fein sympathizer, or some communist to want information from Novak. And, if he refused ..." Fleming made a cutthroat sign using his left hand.

"Ian, I'm a simple police officer. I follow the evidence. I don't offer theories that don't have any evidence."

Fleming waved to the waitress and asked for coffee. He looked at Lundin's cup and said to the waitress, "Two, please." When she returned and had filled their coffee cups, he said, "So what evidence do we have? We have a man murdered using a technique taught at the school. We had a sea chest with history which someone was so determined to acquire that they almost killed you earlier this evening. And you have a strange Biblical quote about revenge. Did I miss anything?"

"We have an instructor and a medical staff who wanted me to think Novak drowned. And, we have a very nervous supervisor at HYDRA who I intend to question tomorrow." Lundin suddenly realized Fleming had once again conjured up a partnership that was not the Mountie way. He shook his head and said, "I need some sleep. I must make a call early in the morning to the chief inspector." Lundin looked at Fleming. "Are you willing to stick with me on this project?"

"Miles, this has been the best day I've had since I arrived. I'm sure the staff would be happy to have me disappear … perhaps permanently. And, there are only a few days left in the training class. After that, the students who pass will head to England for advanced training. If any of them are part of this case, we must get to the bottom of this in the next four days."

With that Fleming stood up and headed for the staircase and his room. Lundin noticed that Fleming had left him to pay the bill. He also noticed Fleming walked as if he had drunk nothing but coffee. He shook his head and said, "Whatever he might be, Fleming is no toff." He pulled out his wallet and waved to the waitress.

She approached and said, "No sir. Commander Fleming paid the bill in advance."

Lundin was left wondering about his new "partner" and how a Navy staff officer had learned so much about this shadow world of Camp X.

The Investigation: Day Three
The more you know, the less you understand

16 October 1942, Camp X and Oshawa

CHAPTER TEN — PARTNERSHIP OVER BREAKFAST

undin walked down the stairs toward the hotel restaurant. It was 0600hrs and he assumed he could have a quiet breakfast before making the call to the chief inspector. He also assumed that after last night's excesses, Fleming would be in bed for some hours. That last assumption was completely wrong. He found Fleming in the restaurant tucking into a large breakfast of eggs, sausage, bacon, toast and coffee. He said, "What, no pancakes?"

Fleming looked up, wiped his lips with a napkin and said, "Not yet. Did you decide to sleep in after our evening?"

Lundin nodded. "Yes, I usually get up well before six but I thought I might be a little self-indulgent today."

"Sarcasm does you no favors, Miles. The truth is I couldn't sleep much last night, so I came down here and the morning staff took pity on me when they arrived at 5 a.m. I hope you don't mind that I didn't wait for you."

"Not at all." He waved to the waitress and said, "Ma'am, I would like some coffee and pancakes with a fried egg on top and bacon on the side, please." The waitress nodded and headed back to the kitchen.

"So, what's on the agenda today, Miles?"

"I thought I would get you back to camp so you don't miss out on the last of the training and then I would visit the coroner who, I might add, did a very thorough job."

"You aren't getting rid of me that easily! There are only four days left for the selection class. Long before you arrived, the cadre, from the commander down to Creed, made it clear I was not going to participate in the final problem. I could watch some from a distance, I could watch their staff at the command cell, but I could not interfere, as they told me, in the training success or failure of the participants."

Fleming lighted a cigarette and blew smoke toward the ceiling. "The thought of sitting in the back of the room for four days while receiving hateful stares from the instructors seems to me about as enjoyable as four days in a dentist's chair. No, thank you! I had planned on clearing my room and leaving today for Toronto, taking the train to the coast and then on to the first Royal Navy ship headed back across the Atlantic. If you will allow me to continue to travel with you, I would be most obliged. At this point, I am captured by the fact that we might be on the trail of a German assassin."

Lundin's coffee and breakfast arrived. He took a bit of time over his plate to consider the risks versus gains by continuing to work with Fleming. After all, he was an amateur with no background in investigation. On the other hand, he was a Royal Navy officer and had already proven his usefulness in revealing facts related to the victim. Finally, Lundin realized that if he irritated Fleming, he might irritate both the Royal Navy and Stephenson and that irritation would mean he would irritate Chief Inspector McClellan. "Ian, you need to know you have no authority here in Canada and I will need to be the primary investigator." He took a sip of coffee from the white ceramic mug. "However, if you are willing to be an advisor, that would be excellent."

Fleming smiled and said, "I told you that I've always been an outsider, so I will be happy to be your outside advisor."

"Good. Then here is my plan for the day. First, I will drop you off at the camp. Collect your things and make a point to the powers that be that you are off to the Admiralty. Arrange for a car to bring you back here. Do your best to convince them you saw what you needed to see and you want to get out of their way as they finish their selection process. While you are doing that, I will make a call to my chief inspector and provide him with an update. We can meet here and go to the coroner's office. Agreed?"

"Miles, agreed! However, may I suggest…?"

Lundin could see this would be an imperfect relationship. It was not exactly the Force protocol, but he nodded.

"I would not make the call to your chief inspector from the camp. Unless, of course, you want every one of your suspects to know what you know and what you think. The camp phones are all monitored, and the entire staff will know your thoughts shortly after you say them. There is certainly an assassin in the camp and, to my mind, that assassin is a spy. I think the only way to catch said villain is to keep your report out of the ears of those at the camp."

"So, call from here?"

"Miles, there are things you need to learn about the shadow world. If the camp is not secure, how in the world do you think the hotel is any more secure? The camp leadership drink in the Hideout when classes are not in session. I think the walls will have ears, if you under-stand my meaning."

Lundin did not appreciate being lectured, but he had to admit Fleming had a point. "Ian, what are you recommending?"

"First, I will find my own way back to camp using a local taxi. Second, I recommend you go out on the street and use one of the phone boxes here in Oshawa. We don't let the camp know we are working together and we don't let them know what you have found out so far. And …" Fleming paused to finish his coffee, "… I don't think it is in your interest at this point to let your chief inspector know that an amateur sleuth from British Naval Intelligence is helping. It will muddy the waters."

With that, Fleming stood and said, "It's your turn to pay. I'm heading back to camp. When do we regroup?"

Lundin looked at his watch. It was 0630hrs. "Can you get there and back before ten?"

"I'll be here drinking coffee by half nine. Whenever you are free, I will be ready to go."

"OK, see you then."

Lundin let out a long breath. Fleming was certainly helpful, but he also had too much energy for the sort of investigation that Lundin was used to in the RCMP. Fleming made too many leaps of faith, and he clearly already had the sort of perpetrator in mind even if he didn't know the name of said perpetrator. Lundin preferred a deliberate building of evidence before he decided who might be the villain. He waved to the waitress and asked for more coffee, then pulled out his notebook and started to write what evidence he did have. When the waitress returned with the coffee, he asked her, "Where is the nearest phone booth?"

Lundin barely fit in the phone booth. The Canadian telephone system had yet to build out many of these public telephones and those they did were old, wooden affairs with folding doors designed to keep out the weather. Lundin's shoulders required him to angle his body against one wall as he dialed his Toronto headquarters. As he waited for the dispatcher to track down the chief inspector, he looked at his notebook. He had five bullet points that he wanted to say:

As the chief inspector had warned, camp personnel were secretive and openly lied to him about the cause of death;

Nearly everyone in the camp had the skills necessary to murder Novak;

Novak had a sensitive job, based on a communications channel between London and the US;

Novak was a radio operator with the Commandos before coming to the camp;

Other than Novak, so far there were three Canadians worth tracing: Petyr Jovanovic, Ken Stevens and Beatrice Thomas. He doubted there would be anything important to the investigation, but he learned long ago that you never knew what might be useful.

The conversation went as he had expected. He relayed the points and expanded on them if McClellan wanted further details. He explained his plan to meet with the coroner and then meet again with Novak's supervisor, Ken Stevens. He intended to spend the day expanding his understanding of Novak's life at the camp and he hoped that would reveal something that would narrow down the field of potential villains. He decided to raise the possibility that this was about Novak's sensitive job rather than some personal grudge. He did so carefully and only as a secondary possibility.

McClellan's response was curt. "Lundin, don't go looking for shadows! There are plenty of them in that secret world, eh? Find a common-sense reason for this murder. You know the drill: greed, drink, jealousy over work or jealousy over a woman. If you eliminate those possibilities, then we can start thinking about other possibilities. Understood?"

Lundin responded clearly. "Yes, sir."

"Alright then. It sounds like you have a full day ahead of you. Are you staying at the camp?"

"No sir. They didn't offer and I didn't ask. I'm staying at the Hotel Genosha in Oshawa, room 22. I thought a little distance might be useful."

"Well done, Lundin. That camp is filled with secrets and you don't know what might happen if you had to live with those … people."

"Yes sir."

"Get to work then, and call me tomorrow."

Lundin said, "Yes sir," knowing that McClellan had already hung up. He put his notebook back in his left breast pocket, opened the door and walked away from the booth. He put on his Stetson and let out a breath. He hoped the day would give him something, anything, to make this investigation easier. However, his own view of the case and of Camp X was sufficiently muddled that he wasn't sure what would happen next.

CHAPTER ELEVEN — A CONVERSATION IN THE BUICK

Fleming was waiting when Lundin returned to the hotel. For the first time, he was wearing his Royal Navy uniform, with the gold braid on the sleeve that signified his rank as well as his reserve officer status. He had a single row of ribbons, none of which made any sense to Lundin. His shoes were polished bright, as was the brim of his white officer's cap. Lundin was suitably impressed. His first impressions of Fleming as a fop were changing over time. It was clear that Fleming was a chameleon. He could present himself as an insouciant member of the British elite, as a commando trainee, and now as a formal member of the Royal Navy elite. He could change his demeanor as easily as he could change his clothes. Lundin wasn't sure why Fleming decided to be a Navy commander today, but he had no doubt he would find out.

They loaded into Lundin's Buick and headed to the address listed for the Oshawa coroner. In October, sunrise came late, and as they headed east the sun glinted off the navy-blue dash. When he was in the Northwest Territories, Lundin always had sunglasses to wear to avoid snow blindness. He regretted not packing them as he squinted into the sun. Even at his best Lundin was not a talkative man, and he was not at his best. He was frustrated that there were dozens of questions but few answers, and that he didn't have many options left to explore.

The coroner was one and Novak's supervisor was another. He held out little hope that the RCMP would find any information on the

Canadians, and he wasn't sure that the correspondent named Novosel was even part of the equation. As these frustrations rumbled around in his head, he looked out over the long hood of the Buick and did his best to avoid the potholes in the road to the coroner. Adding to his frustration was Fleming, seated next to him on the cloth bench seat of the Buick. Fleming seemed to be a person who simply couldn't accept companionable silence as an option while riding in a car. It wasn't that his comments weren't focused on the investigation. It was just that Lundin needed quiet, and he wasn't going to get it with Fleming by his side.

"Miles, I was thinking about the case." Fleming paused to see if he was going to get affirmation that Lundin was interested in his thoughts. Lundin's silence didn't dissuade him from continuing. "So, to my way of thinking there are two possibilities. Either he was murdered because of his current job or he was murdered because of his past. His current job is very sensitive, and would be just the thing the Nazis might want to exploit. If they approached him and he said no, they would have to kill him. See?"

Lundin's silence continued.

"OK, so the other possibility is something to do with his past. His job on the Campbeltown had to be based on some other contact with the Commandos. After all, he was pulled from one destroyer to another more sensitive operation for some reason. So, if there was something from his past that finally caught up with him that might explain his murder. For example, you talked about Novosel. What if Novosel is a commando?"

Lundin finally accepted that Fleming wouldn't stop talking unless he said something. He said, "Let's just say there was a Nazi spy who killed Novak. How did he get into the camp? It isn't easy to walk in."

"No, but it isn't hard to come by boat."

Lundin thought for a moment. That would explain Novak's body in the water. It still was a stretch to think that a Nazi somehow approached Novak out of the blue. "So, how did Novak come in contact with this Nazi?"

"Maybe he had long contact with the Nazi during his time with the Royal Navy."

Lundin thought Fleming had an active imagination and was using that imagination to create a complex plot right out of a mystery novel. He said, "Ian, 'maybe' is not a word we like to use in the Mounties. We need some facts to drive the investigation."

Lundin's comment seemed only to accelerate the Englishman's thought process. "You are saying we need more information on Novak and Novosel, eh? Perhaps I can get some of that from Room 39."

"Eh?"

"Where I work, Miles. Room 39 is the office designation for Royal Navy Intelligence. You would be surprised how much we know about the Admiralty, the Combined Operations units and, for that matter, Nazi spies."

"And how do we get them to help? Do you just call the office and ask?"

Fleming smiled and said, "Yes, that's precisely what I intend to do. I will use HYDRA."

Lundin could only say, "Oh my." Luckily they pulled up at the doctor's office, the conversation ending as they got out and walked to the house of the coroner.

CHAPTER TWELVE — DOCTOR'S VISIT

D r. James Sutton's house on 9420 King's Road was a well-kept, white plank, two-story house perched on a small hill overlooking Lake Ontario. The house was just far enough outside the city of Oshawa to be private, but not so far outside town to be surrounded by farmland and grazing cattle. There was a deep porch in the front and a small garden bounded by a stone fence that encircled the house. Autumn weather had already withered the garden, but Lundin recognized rosebushes and another vine, perhaps a honeysuckle? The house was recently painted a brilliant white with navy-blue shutters. Lundin could imagine a former Navy officer spending summer afternoons on his porch using binoculars to watch the freighters and sailboats on the lake. He also suspected that in the winter, the doctor might close those blue shutters to keep out the wind and the spray from the lake. Lundin decided that the homeowner must be a man of some precision and diligence. It would not be easy to keep a garden so close to the lake where winter lasted long after the calendar said it was spring.

They parked in the stone driveway and got out of the Buick. Fleming said, "Did you call to let him know we are coming?"

Lundin shook his head as he put on his Stetson. "Yes, Ian. I did make an appointment. Dr. Sutton should be expecting us."

Chastised, Fleming said, "I just wanted to be sure he would be home."

They walked side by side to the porch, climbed the three steps and approached the door. Before Lundin could knock, the door opened.

A tall, thin man in a full three-piece wool suit greeted them. "Gentlemen, welcome to my home. I hope you like tea. I have some made, with biscuits I made this morning."

As they followed Sutton into his house, Fleming whispered, "I hate tea."

Lundin whispered back, "You will bloody well take tea, Ian."

The house followed a pattern that Lundin had seen across Canada. The entrance opened to a hallway with stairs going to the second floor and doors opening to the left and the right. If the house followed the norm, Lundin expected the room to the left was the parlor and the room to the right was a study or library. Perhaps in this case, it would be the doctor's surgery. Behind the two rooms would be a kitchen to the left and a toilet to the right. Sutton turned at the first door to the right and entered a room with dark maple bookshelves on all four walls. Rather than being used as a surgery, the room was best described as a library with a large desk near a pair of floor-to-ceiling windows and four leather chairs bordering a Persian carpet.

In the middle of the carpet was a simple oak table set with three white-ceramic tea mugs with a Royal Navy insignia, along with sugar and milk and a teapot under an embroidered tea cozy. A small plate of biscuits sat next to the teapot. Paintings of sailing ships and two photos of Navy ships were placed carefully on the top shelves of the bookcases. Hanging on the wall behind the desk were Sutton's diploma from medical school and his Royal Navy commission. Lundin expected the house was fully electrified, but there were three kerosene lamps placed around the room on small tables.

Sutton motioned for them to sit in the chairs facing the windows. The doctor sat with his back to the glass, where light from outdoors created a halo effect around his bald head. He said, "I will play mother if that is satisfactory." Sutton didn't wait for any comment as he poured three cups of very black tea. "Milk or sugar?"

Fleming was the first to respond. "Black tea, sir." Sutton nodded and handed him a full mug of tea.

Lundin said, "Black with some sugar, please."

Sutton delivered a mug with tea the color of caramel and then poured himself a mug of tea, adding nothing at all. He sat back. "Help yourselves to the biscuits. It was what I had on hand this morning."

Lundin opened the conversation. "Sir, thank you for taking the time with us. It is an important part of the investigation and, to be blunt, your report is the only real set of facts we have yet on the murder."

Sutton preened at the compliment. "It is my pleasure, gentlemen. I wonder if you could explain why a Royal Navy commander is part of the investigation."

Lundin took the first stab at an answer. "As you probably already know, the camp is a sensitive military site, and it turns out Commander Fleming was there for another reason. He has been kind enough to offer his assistance."

Sutton nodded. "Of course, it has nothing to do with Commander Fleming finding the body, eh? Keep your friends close and your enemies closer?"

Fleming almost choked on his tea. He offered, "The Royal Navy is hardly the enemy in this case, sir."

"I expect not. I understand you are from Room 39. Most hush-hush."

It was Lundin's turn to be surprised. "Sir, how do you know of Commander Fleming's role in the case or, for that matter, his assignment in the Admiralty?"

Sutton waved a hand in dismissal of the question. "The Royal Navy officer corps is relatively small, and the connections run long and deep. I saw the initial report and wondered about Commander Fleming. It didn't take long for me to find out he was Rear Admiral Godfrey's aide. You see, I am a former shipmate of Admiral Hall."

Lundin looked puzzled, so Fleming explained. "Admiral Hall was Admiral Godfrey's predecessor during the Great War. I believe he had a hand in my appointment."

Sutton nodded. "Got it in one, Commander Fleming."

Lundin was beginning to wonder if he would ever get the focus back to the investigation if these two Navy officers started to reminisce on the world of Naval Intelligence. He started gently, "Sir, your report was very detailed. Are you the county coroner and, if so, do you see many murder cases?"

"Staff Sergeant Lundin, I am not really the official coroner. Rather, I am considered a special assistant to the coroner on sensitive cases. I was asked to consult on the case by Vice Admiral Percy Nelles."

Fleming interjected, "Chief of the Canadian Naval Staff."

"Percy's staff told the coroner that Novak was a member of the Navy and he wanted a Navy man to be the coroner. He asked the Canadian Minister of Defense, who asked Mr. Stephenson, who asked, politely of course, that I might be involved. The rest, as they say, was history."

Lundin smiled. "I believe that is how I ended up on the investigation."

"Navy man, then?"

"No, sir. A soldier in the Great War, but apparently known to the seniors in Ottawa."

"That means we must solve this crime."

Both Fleming and Lundin spoke at the same time, "Yes, sir."

Sutton looked up at them both. "You said you've seen my report."

Lundin nodded. "That's why we're here."

"So, then you know that Novak was killed with a very sophisticated killing technique. Someone trained in the art of close combat. Perhaps a single blow to stun him, and then …" Sutton put down his mug and made a wrenching movement with both hands moving in opposite directions. "It isn't easy to snap a neck. Much easier ways to kill a man, but if you know what you are doing, it is very quick and silent. I suppose it is how you silence a sentry."

Lundin was beginning to realize Sutton knew more about Camp X than he had admitted. His thoughts went first to the Official Secrets Act paperwork, and then to whether he wanted Sutton to know what they knew about the camp and camp personnel. Before he had a chance to structure the next set of questions, Fleming interrupted his opening gambit.

"Yes, sir. And consistent with what they are teaching the students at the camp."

Sutton looked at Lundin and said, "Senior Sergeant, don't look so dismayed. Virtually the entire county knows that the camp is training Canadian commandos. It is not a secret, no matter what the Canadian or British governments think. Now, what more do you want to know from me?"

Lundin decided it was time to lay his cards down and ask direct questions. "Sir, I would like to know two things: First, was the murderer left or right-handed? Second, could a woman or a man of small stature have accomplished this?"

"May I call you by your given name, please?"

"Certainly, Doctor. My name is Miles."

"Miles, the answer to your first question must be a best guess, not a statement of fact. Given the way the neck was twisted, I would guess that the attacker was left-handed." Sutton stood up and said, "Commander Fleming, if you would be so kind as to allow me to demonstrate?"

Fleming stood up and said, "Absolutely, sir."

"Now," Sutton continued, "if the attacker was right-handed, he would have placed his left arm around Novak like so." He came behind Fleming, wrapped his entire left arm around Fleming's neck with the crook of his elbow tight against his windpipe. "He would then grab the chin with his right hand like so and wrench as hard as possible." He placed his hand over Fleming's chin and pulled gently. He then released Fleming from his grip. "In fact, the torsion on the neck was in the opposite direction, arguing a left-handed grip. Given the damage to the back of Novak's neck, I suspect he was hit very hard there first to stun him. Once stunned, he could have been on his hands and knees. To answer your second question, in that position any man or woman with the right training could accomplish the act."

Lundin nodded. "Doctor, can you imagine some reason why the medical team at the camp didn't come to the same conclusion?"

"Miles, it seems clear to me that the camp leadership did not want anyone to know that Novak was murdered in this or any other manner. Easier to dismiss the case as an accidental drowning, or even a case of some local drowning a man on purpose or by accident. When you complete a report as I did, you are pointing a finger directly at camp personnel." Sutton returned to his tea.

Lundin said, "Do you know who asked the coroner to do a second evaluation?"

"Novak's supervisor. A gentleman named …"

Fleming jumped in, "Stevens."

"Yes, that's right. Stevens. A mousey man, if I can offer an impolite evaluation. But he was adamant that the county coroner look at Novak's body. I suspect he was the one who forced the issue up to Ottawa and the Canadian Navy. I only met Stevens once when I visited the mortuary. Stevens looked most distressed."

"Distressed?"

"It seemed to me that Stevens felt responsible. I don't know if he felt responsible because Novak worked for him or because he knew something about the murder. Gentlemen, that is your business."

Fleming said, "Sir, that is precisely our business, and we will get to the bottom of this."

"You know, Novak was a Navy man. He served with the Canadian fleet and, I believe, with the Royal Navy. After facing the terrors of war he did not deserve this."

Lundin said, "Sir, in my experience the victims of violent crime never deserve this."

Sutton nodded. "Quite."

One lesson Lundin learned early in his Mountie career was to always ask a final, open question of any witness. You never knew what might come out. He asked, "Sir, can you think of anything else that might help us?"

Sutton looked Lundin in the eyes and said, "Yes, Miles. I think I have something that you might find most curious, and I think it somehow matters. I can't make any sense out of it, but you might be able to do so."

Sutton walked over to his desk, opened his desk drawer and handed Lundin an American silver dollar. Lundin held it in his hand, noting the weight was slightly more than most dollars. Silver dollars were always heavy, but this one was about the same as the one-pound lead shot that he used in his fishing tackle. He said, "Doctor, where did you find this?"

"As you already know, the camp personnel simply identified Novak and assumed or decided to report that he drowned. When Stevens insisted on an autopsy, they drove Novak's body to the mortuary. I already related how I was included in the autopsy. When I arrived, Novak was still dressed and still soaked from some hours in the lake." Sutton paused and looked at Lundin. "I suppose you realize the first step in a formal autopsy for an unexplained death is to systematically disrobe the victim and check from the top of his head to the soles of his feet for injuries that might help investigators. Oshawa is a small place. The coroner and I did the autopsy on our own. There were no assistants or witnesses from the camp. It wasn't my first experience with a violent death and, honestly, during the Great War I handled many wounded and dead."

Lundin nodded and waited patiently as the doctor paused. He knew he had to let the doctor tell the story in a manner that would make sense to him rather than providing details that would be exclusively important to Lundin.

Fleming was less patient and spoke. "Doctor, where did you find this strange artifact?" Lundin gave Fleming a hard look. He wanted to ask the same question, but he also wanted a context for the answer. He was afraid Fleming's use of what investigators called a "closed question" would produce only the most basic answer rather than an answer that provided the context. Fleming noticed the look. "Sorry, Doctor. I shouldn't have interrupted."

Sutton continued. "As I said, my first step was to disrobe Novak. When I came to his shoes, I untied them and pulled them off. As I pulled off his left shoe, this item came out from the interior of his shoe. It wasn't hard to miss since it made quite a ringing noise as it fell to the floor. I decided for reasons I still can't explain not to list the disc in my official report."

Lundin asked, "Did you find any other odd items or odd marks on Novak other than those you have already mentioned?"

"No other mysterious items, but it was clear that just before his neck was broken he was struck twice. I assume the first strike was in the left kidney about two inches below his ribcage. The second was, as I mentioned before, most probably the heel of a hand against his jaw. I suppose the attacker intended the second blow to stun Novak, allowing him to use the technique I described before."

"Best guess on what was used in the strike to the kidney?"

"Certainly not anything hard like a nightstick or a hammer. That would have left a much deeper bruise, or even a cut. I believe that both strikes were open-hand strikes. Not punches exactly, but certainly more than a slap."

Fleming looked at Lundin, who nodded. Fleming said, "The close-combat training includes use of open-hand strikes both with the heel of the hand and a knife-edge hand strike. The use of the fist is not recommended simply because you can break your hand the first time you punch someone."

Lundin had seen enough bar fights — and been involved in a few — to know that punching with a fist was unwise unless you had gloves to cushion the shock to your hand.

Sutton nodded. "Most probably the heel of the hand for both."

Fleming asked, "Miles, may I see the dollar?" Lundin handed the piece over to Fleming. He placed it in the palm of his right hand and placed the palm of his left hand covering the dollar. He then rotated his left hand clockwise, producing a small squeak from his hands. He raised his left hand and then slowly unscrewed the top of the dollar from the bottom. He stopped before separating the two halves. "It really is easy once you know the trick. The dollar has been milled with a very fine thread that is counterintuitive. Even if you thought there was some sort of thread on the two halves, you would assume it would unscrew like any other threaded tool you have ever used. That is, tightening clockwise, loosening anti-clockwise. If you tried that technique, you would be disappointed because nothing would happen."

Sutton smiled at Fleming. "A war secret?"

Fleming nodded. "Doctor, as you know from the Great War, we always do our best to encourage captured prisoners of war to escape and return to the forces. In this war, with so many of our soldiers and airmen trapped in occupied Europe, we have created a special unit to help evaders. Our airmen and commandos are given small escape and evasion survival kits. Most are just common-sense items disguised in their clothes. If they must hide a special item, a compass for example, it is often hidden in something that would survive an initial search."

Sutton said, "Like the sole of a shoe?"

"Well, more like what you identified, a cavity on the inside of the shoe that would be hard to find." Fleming looked at Lundin. "Shall we see what Novak was hiding in this little device?"

Lundin smiled. "Well, since you are playing the magician, I think it is only right that you make the reveal."

Fleming completed unscrewing the top half of the disk and lifted it off. He placed the top shell on Sutton's desk and reached into the small, revealed cavity. He pulled out two pieces of tissue paper. On the first was a series of numbers and letters in five columns and ten rows. The numbers and letters were barely visible to the naked eye. On the second paper was a very small map of the lake front at the camp with three marks identifying specific locations along the shoreline.

Lundin nodded. "X marks the spot, eh?"

Sutton said, "Buried treasure?"

Fleming smiled and said, "Doctor, much more likely buried secrets."

CHAPTER THIRTEEN — A MEETING AT HYDRA

They drove in silence for most of the way back to the camp. Finally, Lundin said, "Spies?"

"Likely spies or saboteurs. However, you need to know that part of the instruction at the camp includes impersonal communications with agents. What that means is you use what is called a dead drop. You drop a message at a location, then you leave. The agent goes to that location at another time, picks up the message and either delivers his own message using the same technique or follows your instructions. My guess is that's the use of the concealment."

"Any chance it could be some sort of prank?"

"The sort of thing I might do?"

Lundin looked away from the road for a moment and stared at Fleming. "Well, it crossed my mind."

Fleming laughed. "There were days before the war that I would have done something like that. My brother Peter and I often sent coded messages to each other when we were boys. But, I never created such a clever way to conceal a message. I may be a lot of things, but one thing I am not is a machinist. Did you see how well the pieces fit together?"

"Yes. You would need real skill and a machine shop to make that happen. Are there machinists and a machine shop in the camp?"

"Most certainly. They create all sorts of challenges for the students. Think about how complicated that house of horrors is with its pop-up targets, smoke and fireworks. And for that matter, think about how complicated it must be to keep HYDRA running. You need more than radio operators to make HYDRA work."

"I was thinking the same thing myself. One winter when I was stationed in Yellowknife, I was snowbound for about a week. I had a wireless set to communicate with Edmonton and took a basic course before I headed north of 60 to be sure I could make some repairs. I even took a small kit to make my own crystal radio set so I could listen to radio stations. I found out early on that radio repair was not my forte."

"North of 60?"

"The Northwest Territories are all north of 60 degrees north latitude. When you leave the provinces for the north, the shorthand comment is you are going north of 60."

"So, did you keep wireless contact with your superiors in Edmonton?"

"Ian, I called few in the Edmonton office my superiors."

"Apologies. Your supervisors, then?"

"No. The wireless stopped working in mid-October that year when the temperatures started to drop. I decided I would be better off just doing my duty without supervision."

"Miles, I like the way you think."

"I'm assuming that is how you decided to take the training at the camp."

"Well, I did ask the admiral. He often lets me pursue an idea, whether it is good or not. He just said I was not to get injured during my month away and I could stop thinking that I would be a character out of John Buchan."

"I always liked *The Thirty-Nine Steps.*"

"I'm much more of a fan of *Greenmantle.*"

Lundin shook his head. "I'm not surprised."

When they approached the gate, Lundin said, "I intend to interview Novak's supervisor on my own."

"Absolutely. Plus, I need to get inside HYDRA so that I can communicate with my people in Room 39. Last night I called them and arranged approvals so I can enter the inner sanctum."

"Just stay clear of anyone who looks like he might put his arm around your neck."

Fleming paused to finish the last drag of his cigarette. "I promise."

Unlike the previous day's foolishness with the gate guards, once they saw Lundin and Fleming in the vehicle, they opened the gate and offered a formal salute. Lundin said, "I guess there is an advantage having a Royal Navy officer in the car."

"After what I heard about your problems yesterday, I think there is an advantage to having an RCMP Mountie driving."

"You heard?"

"It's a small camp, and we don't have a lot to talk about amongst ourselves. Every student is regularly quizzed on what they told other students. You can gossip, but you can't reveal anything about yourself." Fleming shook his head. "Except for me, of course. They all talk to me because I am both one of them and not one of them. They see how the camp trainers treat me, so they know I'm not a fink in their midst. The word was that the camp guards didn't even respond to you until Creed arrived. Must have been most annoying, eh?"

"It was that. I didn't hear what Creed told them, but as we drove into the camp they were still doing press-ups."

"Well, they are just kids. Most are just out of their basic training and waiting for replacement assignments in the Canadian First Division. They might have thought it would be the only time they could be rude to a Mountie."

"They were about to learn a small lesson when Creed arrived."

"Miles, I'm an Englishman and even I know you are never rude to a Mountie."

Lundin stopped the Buick in front of HYDRA and they both got out. The two guards at the door came to the position of attention. Fleming rendered a salute and said, "Please tell Mr. Stevens that Senior Staff Sergeant Lundin has arrived for his interview and that Commander Fleming has arrived to communicate to London."

One of the guards did an about-face and entered the building. While they were waiting another MP arrived from around the corner of the building. He looked nearly 50 years old and was not in the best of shape. While his uniform fit poorly, everything that should be polished was polished and everything that should be creased was creased. He was definitely a veteran. Lundin also noticed the master sergeant's stripes resting just below the white armband that identified him as a military policeman. He showed considerable surprise when he noticed Fleming. He stopped, came to the position of attention and rendered a very formal salute. Fleming returned the salute as the sergeant approached. Lundin took over. He offered his hand and said, "Lundin, RCMP."

The sergeant looked relieved. "Jasper, reserve provost marshal office. We manage the security here."

Lundin only needed the answer to one question, so he chose not to use his normal warm up discussion. Instead, he simply said, "Master Sergeant Jasper, what time does your guard mount change each afternoon?"

"Sergeant, we change shift every four hours starting at midnight. I change the night guard mount at 2000hrs and then again at 2400hrs. The men walking the perimeter change places with the door guards two hours into the shift."

"As you already know, I'm investigating the death of the HYDRA night shift supervisor, Edward Novak. I wondered if it would be possible for Novak to have left the building before the shift change and the new shift might not know he was gone. It looks to me as if they are not regularly checking inside the building."

"Correct. I will be honest in saying I was surprised that Novak was found in the lake. The detail at HYDRA just assumed he was inside. All the wireless operators come out from time to time, just to get fresh air and to take a break from the hum of that equipment. We don't keep a log of when they go in or out. Our remit is simply to keep outsiders out, not to keep insiders in."

Lundin smiled and said, "I suspected as much, but you know how investigations go. Sometimes you must ask dumb questions just to make sure you have your i's dotted and your t's crossed."

"Don't I know it! This is a tedious bit of work for the men. They want to go to war. I saw war in the trenches the last time. I don't mind tedium."

"I'm with you. My days in the trenches are still with me and I don't want to repeat them. I'm sorry I brought you out for this, but I needed to be sure."

"Not a problem, Lundin. I needed to visit the men anyhow and 1700hrs is as good a time as any."

Lundin offered his hand, Jasper took it and then marched off in the direction of his jeep.

Fleming said, "Just dotting the i's?"

"I could see he didn't know much, and I just didn't want to have him leave angry. Believe me, no one wants an angry master sergeant."

"I'll make a note."

Stevens came out just as Jasper disappeared in his jeep. Lundin was left with the impression that Stevens had been waiting at the door. He waved them both in and the guards closed the door.

Inside HYDRA, there were racks of communications gear. It was warm inside, and there was a loud hum from the tubes used to drive the radio gear. Five men sat at different workstations, wearing headsets and completely oblivious of their arrival. In front of them were large pads of paper and a Morse code key. Two of the men were using their keys and the others were feverishly writing down incoming messages. After a day outdoors and in the coroner's cold house, Lundin immediately started to sweat. In his previous meeting with Stevens, he thought Stevens was sweating because he was nervous. Now he realized it was the fact that Stevens worked in a hothouse warm enough to grow tropical plants. Of course, there was no room for plants with the racks and racks of equipment.

Fleming demonstrated a degree of insouciance that must fascinate his fellow students and frustrate the senior military officers at Camp X. He unbuttoned his Navy jacket and took it off. He rolled up his sleeves and said in an offhand way, "Ken, where can I send and receive my communications?" Lundin thought Fleming's comment sounded like a friend asking his host if he could use the telephone. Of course, HYDRA wasn't exactly a phone and Stevens wasn't a friend. Still, the way Fleming framed the question, it seemed as if it would be rude if Stevens tried to be anything but a good host.

"Commander, I set up a small table in the corner for your communications. Do you need one of my men to send and receive?"

"Thanks, Ken, but I have the necessary skills. I'm not as deft as your men, but I can do the needful and my folks back at Room 39 are used to my fist."

Lundin raised an eyebrow. Fleming turned to him and said, "All communicators have a distinctive way of using the Morse key. It is called their fist. I am a bit slow-witted with the key, so the folks in Room 39 have referred to my fist as soft. I don't think that is meant as a compliment."

Stevens said, "One last thing, Commander. Please don't smoke in here. It's not really a regulations issue, it's just a fire hazard with all the equipment."

"Righto, Ken. Thanks." With that, Fleming headed to his appointed spot, sat down and started twisting dials to find the proper Royal Navy frequency. Lundin was surprised at how capable this man was. He decided that the insouciance and bonhomie was just a cover for a highly skilled man who was far more than the dilettante he presented to the outside world. Most probably, that was another reason why the camp officers disliked him. Everything came easy to this nimble and quick-witted man.

He turned to Stevens and said, "Mr. Stevens, it there a place where we can have a private talk?"

"Sergeant Lundin, if you don't mind, could we have our talk outside? I so rarely get outside during my shift and, honestly, there isn't any place inside the building where there isn't someone working on something."

Lundin was relieved. He was starting to sweat through his blouse and he didn't want to start sweating through into his wool tunic as well. "After you," he said.

Stevens rolled his sleeves back down and pulled on a well-worn wool suit jacket that wasn't even close to a good match for his wool trousers. In Lundin's experience, that usually meant the man was a bachelor. His socks probably didn't match either.

"Mr. Stevens …"

"Please call me Ken. The camp seniors always call me Mr. Stevens to emphasize I am a civilian, and it can be irksome."

"Absolutely, Ken." Lundin had no intention of offering his first name. This was a formal interview. "I have several questions and will need to take notes. I hope you don't mind."

"Sergeant, I am an engineer by training. I like the idea of precision. Take as many notes as you need."

Lundin opened the top right pocket of his tunic and pulled out his notebook. From his top left pocket, he pulled out a pencil. He looked at his watch and made a note at the top of the first open page. *Stevens. 16 Oct 42, 1518hrs.* He started with what he expected to be an easy first question. "When did Novak start working at HYDRA?"

"Sergeant, that's not easy to answer simply because Ned was here when I arrived this summer. I think he came when HYDRA was first built and stayed on. I arrived this past June and he was already working the day shift with two wireless operators. Before the war, I worked at McGill University teaching electrical engineering. I volunteered in 1940, but I have very poor eyesight and a slight heart condition. No one in the Canadian services wanted any part of me, except …"

Lundin knew that sometimes in an interview you had to coax a person. It was important not to fill in the blank for them but rather to just reinforce the fact you were interested. That could be difficult with Canadians in general, and especially tribal people in the north.

Their reticence wasn't because they were suspicious, they were just reserved. He expected this former professor was just that — reserved. He said, "Except?"

"One day last spring, a man in a Royal Canadian Air Force uniform came to the university and asked if I would travel to New York on a mission for Canada. Well, I was curious, and I didn't have any more classes that week, so I agreed. Can you believe it, he flew me down to New York on a military aircraft!" Lundin could tell that Stevens was dazzled by the trip. He nodded in an effort keep Stevens on track. "I ended up meeting with Mr. Stephenson in his offices in New York. He explained to me the mission of the Office of British Security Cooperation and asked if I would be interested in helping the war effort. I agreed, and they flew me back to Montreal. The same officer took a note from Mr. Stephenson to the university president and then told me to make my way to Oshawa. I took the train and a bus and arrived in town. There was a Canadian military policeman waiting for me, and he took me to the camp."

"Did you know what you would be doing?"

"Mr. Stepheson told me that I would be briefed by Novak when I arrived. I was to be the supervisor here, and to make sure that the communications systems — everything from the wireless sets to the antennas — were operational twenty-four hours a day. I suspect you will find this odd, but I have enjoyed the work though I haven't been off this post since I arrived. This is such a vital part of the war effort, and I am so pleased to be the man who is responsible for it."

"Novak was OK with having you take over?"

"Funny you should ask that. I was most worried that he would feel he had been demoted. Instead, Ned seemed relieved. He was a very good wireless operator, but he had no experience with a system as large as this and absolutely no experience with large antennas. He was a Navy man. The antennas on ships are complicated, but certainly nothing like the antenna field we have here." Stevens waved behind him and Lundin looked at the dozen antennas, each over 30 feet high, with guy-wires and radio wires going back into the building. "You know there are very complex equations needed to make sure each of the radio antennas don't interfere with another. For example…"

Lundin could see the university professor was about to start a lecture. He said, "I'm sure that's true, Ken."

Stevens blushed. "I'm sorry, I do get excited about this work."

"Not a problem, Ken. Let's start with a simple question. Why did you insist on an autopsy for Novak?"

Stevens shook his head and looked down at his shoes. "I didn't want to make a fuss, but when I heard that they were saying that Ned drowned, I knew that wasn't right."

Stevens stopped at that point, and it didn't look like he intended to continue. Lundin realized he was going to have to pull each fact out of Stevens. He didn't think that was because Stevens was lying. Still, it meant that he would have to pull hard to get Stevens to respond. He used a simple question that was perfect for prying open thoughts. "Ken, why did you think that?"

"For two reasons. First, Ned was an excellent swimmer. He told me himself that he went through commando training when he was in the Navy, and that meant swimming with a backpack and a rifle. Second, Ned was teetotal. It wasn't as if he was going to get drunk and fall into the lake. Just not who Ned was."

Lundin was about to say something when Stevens added, "And, I thought the camp commander and his officers were way too quick to dismiss Ned's death as an accident. He was my friend and he worked in HYDRA, which is my responsibility. It just wasn't right."

"How did you get them to agree?"

"They never did."

Stevens looked down at his shoes again. "They told me to mind my own business and let professionals handle Ned's death. As if they are professionals in any manner except as soldiers. I may not be a professional soldier, but I understand the importance HYDRA has to our national security and the importance Ned had in the day-to-day operation. I used the HYDRA network to reach out to INTREPID, that's the code name for Mr. Stephenson's office in New York. I suppose he reached out to Ottawa. It was a risk and I know the camp commander hates me for it, but it was the least I could do for Ned."

Lundin thought for a moment as they slowly walked among the antennas. It was starting to make sense why he was the investigator and why the officers in the camp were so eager to get rid of him. He asked, "Ken, what do you know about Novak's past?"

"He was a radioman on lake ore haulers and joined the Navy in 1939. He was always vague about his work with the Navy. He did say he had worked with the Commandos and trained with them in Scotland. It sounded most interesting, but when I asked for more about that part of his war service, he just said that it was ugly and he would rather forget. I delivered letters to Ned from another commando based in Scotland. Well, I know enough about these things to recognize their post office is in Scotland just like our post office is in Kingston at the Army War College. Simply a post office box in some town. Nothing suggesting it was from a military post or going to a military post. His friend could be anywhere. When I asked him about his friend, he said he probably knew more about this camp than he did."

"What did he mean by that?"

"No idea. He said his friend had served with the SOE in Yugoslavia in 1941, and since our camp was an SOE training base his friend must have gone through something similar in England. He did say they met and were mates on some Navy ship known as the Campbeltown. I suppose it was involved in convoy duty."

Lundin stopped writing for a moment and thought about the various threads starting to come together. Of course, they were yet to weave into a rope that would lead him somewhere, but at least some small pieces of the story were showing promise. He shook his head, thinking that if only he had the letters, it would have made things so much easier. Instead, he was ambushed like some rookie and lost the evidence completely. He decided to turn the discussion in a different direction. "Did Ned have any contact with the people at the training facility?"

"Sergeant, I'm sorry to say I have no idea. Ned worked the night shift, I worked days. We would share a cup of tea between our shifts, talking shop. We focused on what was working, what maintenance needed to be accomplished, and what we might do to make HYDRA better. He would tell me how many messages arrived, their priority and when they were dispatched. I would do the same at the end of my shift. We are a clearing house, and we need to keep strict logs on incoming and outgoing traffic. I liked Ned, but I never talked to him about what he did in his spare time. We both live in the barracks. I'm across the hallway from Ned's room. You might think we were close, but we weren't. That is to my shame."

"Why?"

"Because Ned seemed like a lonely man. He was a religious man, and I always assumed his religion helped him. I am not a man who thinks about those things. I wasn't much of a friend."

Lundin nodded. "Ken, you must not blame yourself for Ned's murder. You had nothing to do with it." He paused, then followed up on Stevens' comments. "Do you have religious services here at the camp?"

"They have an Anglican priest from the Canadian forces serving on the post. I doubt he had anything to do with Ned, since he was Serbian Orthodox. Still, you might ask him. He seems a decent man, even if I often think his views are … shall we say … conservative."

Lundin had met more than his share of conservative men of the cloth, especially up in the Northwest Territories. They were usually clueless about their congregation, but a good investigator never ignored a lead. "His name?"

"Captain Jason Jenkins. I think he served in the Great War and was mobilized just to handle recruit training and other duties here in Canada. Before '39, he was an Anglican vicar in Oshawa."

"Thanks. Shall we head back to HYDRA?"

"Sergeant, thanks for taking Ned's death seriously. You are the only one who is doing so. Ned deserved better."

"No promises, Ken, but I will do everything in my power to find Novak's killer and bring him to justice. It is what I do."

"That's all I could ask for in this terrible case. I'm not a violent man, and I haven't seen violence in my life. During the Great War, I helped design wireless radios for our ships and for our soldiers. I spent the war in a factory. No shot and shell for me. Suddenly a man I knew is the victim of a violent death. I want to know why."

Lundin had seen more than his share of death. Sometimes he thought he might get used to the violence. In fact, he never had. Not from the war in the trenches over 20 years ago, and not over the years investigating murders across Canada. He hoped he would never accept violence as a normal happening.

"Ken, you never get used to a violent death," he said. "You always have the same question: why? It is my job to answer that question no matter who the victim is or where the violence happens. The victim deserves justice, and their family and friends deserve answers."

Lundin realized he had never articulated these reasons for life as a Mountie. He was slightly embarrassed that he sounded like a recruiting poster, but it was the best he could come up with to comfort Stevens.

Stevens was looking directly at Lundin when he said, "And that's why you will get the answers."

CHAPTER FOURTEEN — NEWS FROM ROOM 39

Lundin was silent on the drive back to the hotel. He was working over in his mind what Stevens had said about Novak and the officers at the camp. There was a simple answer to why the officers were so hostile to further investigation: embarrassment. Lundin had experienced this in his most recent investigation of the stolen rifles at the Toronto armory. None of the civilians or the officers involved in the armory wanted anything to do with the investigation. At one point, he felt like he did after he returned to Canada after the war. The Spanish flu epidemic was raging, and anyone who had been in Europe — including soldiers who had served on the front — were treated as likely agents of infection.

The same happened with the armory investigation. The closer he came to a solution, the more the armory personnel avoided contact with him. The same for members of the city government and, for that matter, the Toronto police. Of course, in the end he found that the armory personnel weren't guilty of a crime. They were merely guilty of sloth and complacency. They didn't end up in jail, though he thought some of them should have been charged with some crime. They did lose their jobs, but that was hardly justice in his mind.

His best guess at this point was the Camp X officers didn't want to be accused of poor security or some sort of complacency related to HYDRA. Still, there was another possibility: It could be that one of the officers was complicit in the murder or even might be the murderer. After all, Creed made it clear that nearly every person on the STS side of the camp was more than capable of murder. But what would be the motive? It seemed unlikely that Novak's role in the raid on St. Nazaire or his ties to another commando based in Scotland could lead someone to kill him. And then there was the secret message inside the coin. Was Novak a spy? If so, for whom?

Lundin knew enough about the RCMP work against the Nazis to understand that it would be seen as a real stretch if he were to imply that Novak was meeting a Nazi spy on the Lake Ontario shore. He could imagine how the chief inspector would look at him if he raised that possibility in his call tomorrow morning. He needed a lead. He needed some real evidence. So far, the only evidence was the coin. And that wasn't much help at this point.

They were almost to Oshawa when Fleming said, "If you are going to sulk all night, I'm just going to go back to my room and I'll see you in the morning. I thought for certain you might be interested in the news from Room 39 or, for that matter, what I found out inside HYDRA."

Shaken out of his thoughts, Lundin looked at Fleming. "I apologize, Ian. We have lots of information, most of which I can't see is useful. We have some innuendo and some opinions. But, right now we have no leads."

"Here's what I suggest. We go to our rooms, change out of our uniforms and meet at Harry's. We have a whiskey and then we talk through what we know. After that, we have a good meal and talk about what we think, rather than what we know. By the end of the night, I believe we will have some direction to the investigation."

Lundin nodded as he pulled the Buick up in front of their hotel. He said, "I'll meet you in a half hour."

"I'll be waiting with a bourbon in hand."

As promised, Lundin found Fleming in the bar working on a whiskey.

He walked up to the bar and ordered a Canadian Club and soda and whatever whiskey Fleming was drinking. The bartender nodded, pouring his drink. As he walked to the table, he saw Fleming surrounded by a fog of cigarette smoke. In front of him, he had a small notebook with what looked like a diagram Lundin would have drawn in his office in Toronto. He placed both drinks at the table and sat down. "Been busy?"

"I'm just trying to digest what Room 39 offered. It wasn't easy since I had to first receive the Morse code, decipher same and then put it down in something resembling order."

Lundin was only slightly sarcastic as he said, "All in a day's work for a man from Naval Intelligence."

"Well, as a matter of fact, it is just that." Fleming downed the remainder of his previous whiskey and said, "Much obliged for the refill."

"So, are you going to keep your secrets to yourself or let me in on the mysteries of Room 39?"

"Most of these mysteries, as you call them, are simply Navy records of Novak and his pen pal Novosel. Interesting reading, though I admit I'm not sure if it helps at all."

Lundin had to bite his tongue not to offer the standard investigator reply of "Let me be the judge of that." Instead, he took a sip of his drink and decided to open the discussion. "What did Novak's records show?"

"Honestly, precious little more than you got from his sea chest before you were rapped on the head." Fleming watched as Lundin winced at the reminder. "OK, old chap. Remember, you were supposed to be working in a secret and safe compound."

He watched as Lundin acknowledged his point. "Now, the only important thing was after St. Nazaire, Novak returned to England and the SOE worked hard to recruit him away from the Navy. After all, Serbian radio operators are at a premium."

Lundin shook his head. "Why?"

"Sorry, I forgot you aren't aware of SOE operations. They have been supporting the resistance groups in Yugoslavia since late 1940.

Churchill calls the Balkans the soft underbelly of Europe. He thinks that if we can stir up trouble there, then eventually we can head north or west into Italy."

Fleming looked up at Lundin and realized Lundin could care less about what the Prime Minister or anyone else thought of grand strategy. "Here are the basics. There are two resistance groups. The royalists, known as Chetniks, and the communists, known as Partisans. Both groups are supposed to be fighting the German and Italian troops occupying Yugoslavia. As near as we can tell in Room 39, they spend far more time fighting each other. There are precious few Serbs in the UK, and Novak's file came to the attention of the SOE after he returned from the commando raid and was put up for a gong."

"Gong?"

"Sorry, a bit of Navy speak. A medal. Room 39 reported that several of the surviving officers recommended Novak for a distinguished service order for his role in maintaining communications on the Campbeltown until the last minute. Of course, since he was simply a radioman, the award was rejected. Sadly, the Navy is a bit hidebound in that regard. Officers are usually the ones who get the medals. And sailors … well, unless they are killed in action, they only get mentioned in dispatches. As far as Combined Operations headquarters was concerned, he deserved it. As far as the Royal Navy was concerned, he didn't. Room 39 was agnostic." Fleming shook his head.

"The SOE wanted our man. Why didn't they get him?"

"It turns out that another character in our story heard about Novak as well: Stephenson. And, generally speaking, Stephenson's interests trump just about anyone, except possibly M at SOE or C at MI6."

"C?"

"Sorry. The head of MI6 is known as C simply because he signs his dispatches C. It goes back to …"

"Ian, I really don't care. I just needed to know the shorthand."

"More blither on my part, eh?"

"Let's not call it blither. We will just call it not useful to our investigation."

"Fair point. So, Novak ends up in HYDRA. He has a mate called Novosel, who is another Serbian. He is currently in Scotland. Apparently, he has an SOE connection."

"The revenge quote from the Bible?"

"Perhaps, but who is the target of the revenge? Certainly not Novak."

Lundin nodded. There was an idea forming in his head that looked promising, but he needed more information before he would offer it to anyone, including his unofficial partner, Lieutenant Commander Ian Fleming. He said, "Ian, sometimes you don't have to look far to find the target. Murder is really all about a few basic motives: jealousy, greed and revenge. Sometimes murder wasn't the plan. I've investigated plenty of cases where the victim and the murderer were pals. They get into an argument, and one wrong punch ends the story."

"Unlikely in this case, since he was murdered using a technique taught in the school."

"Too true. We will put anger aside for now, though I still wouldn't eliminate it."

"And the items in the silver dollar?"

"Ah, that is still puzzling. Everything Stevens said about Novak suggests he was a true Canadian patriot. Still, our evidence points to some sort of clandestine relationship."

"I haven't seen anything like that before, but I've never been a spy behind lines. I go to the communications room and they open a large code book and that is that." Fleming took a long swallow of his bourbon and lit another cigarette. "If the map and the code list weren't his, why were they on his person?"

"Ian, exactly my thoughts. Again, we come back to the evidence. If that coin wasn't his, how in the world did it end up on him?"

Fleming stood up and said, "I have the answer to that question, but I'm not going to be able to think if we don't get some food. Shall we go to the dining room?"

Lundin stood up as well. Fleming was already walking to the bar. He said over his shoulder, "Another?"

"No, thanks." Years ago, Lundin decided that he had to remain disciplined when he was on the job. When off duty, he could be encouraged to overindulge. On duty, a single drink or a single beer was all he allowed himself. He had seen too many colleagues fall into the trap of drinking well into the night and waking the next day with a hangover and a case still not solved. Dinner would help, as would at least one cup of coffee, perhaps two.

When the food arrived, Lundin looked down at his steak and realized he hadn't eaten since his early breakfast. He was famished. The plate of steak, cottage fries and coleslaw was just the right answer to his grumbling stomach and, he had to admit, his grumbling mind. Fleming had ordered a broiled fish and a baked potato. He picked at his food as he worked on his bourbon. "Not to your liking?" Lundin asked.

Fleming smiled. "Miles, when I get interested in a project my appetite seems to disappear. Before the war, there were plenty of distractions. As they say: wine, women and song. I travelled a bit. Not like my brother Peter, who traveled extensively and made a name for himself as a writer. I will admit I was less disciplined. I was a writer for a couple of newspapers, but that really didn't suit me. I found a job in the city in the financial sector and wasn't very good at that either. Finance work can make you money, and I really do like money. But it is boring to the extreme. Honestly, I thank my lucky stars that I have my current job. It is exciting stuff. I know the crew here think I am just a dog's body for the admiral, but he tasks me to solve problems for him and gives me plenty of leeway to get the job done. I'm not about to be sent behind the lines, but I did have some adventures in France just before the Nazis finished them."

Fleming paused before he cautiously said, "I am having what might be called a good war. I like the adrenaline surges and the fact that in my own little way I am helping the cause. Probably far more than if I was on a ship at sea or a soldier in North Africa."

Lundin nodded. "I know the feeling. The camaraderie in the trenches was something I never found since the Great War. It was awful and grand at the same time. Of course, I didn't like the fear and the artillery and the gas, and I especially didn't like having to bury friends. But somehow you feel more alive when you are about to die."

Fleming said, "You know, I may use that idea sometime."

Lundin couldn't help but offer a sarcastic comment. "I suspect the men in Room 39 have heard that before."

Fleming didn't seem to notice the dig at his personality. He sipped his bourbon. "After the war, the civilians won't know the positive sides of war," he said, reflectively. "In England, they will know the destructive nature of war. The blitz has done great harm to our country. You folk in North America are important to the war effort, but I doubt your civilians will ever understand the war. And those of us who were in the war might forget how profound our contribution was during the war."

"Ian, nothing I've ever done has been profound."

"You are defending your homeland, and you hunt villains. And, probably most importantly, you do it alone and on your own terms. How can that not be considered profound? If I was to describe a man dedicated to something important, I would use you as a model."

"I suspect there are many commandos you have met who are better models."

"Of course. But they always work in teams. They rarely work alone. Mounties always work alone, correct?"

"In the past we were much closer to a military model, with platoons, companies and even battalions. Those days are mostly over. Today, we are usually individuals or, possibly, a pair of Mounties in a remote location."

"So, the risks are great."

Lundin shrugged. "You could always end up dead in a snowbank if that's what you mean. Villains in the north are just as dangerous as any in the cities. The only real difference is there are fewer witnesses."

He finished his plate and realized that Fleming still hadn't really started. He continued while Fleming picked at his fish, "Not many stories of derring-do in real life. Just hunting men who decided it was easier to steal than to work or easier to murder than to get along with their fellow Canadians. Most times my job isn't like some mystery novel, sorting out who did the crime. It is more often assembling the facts so that I can arrest the perpetrator. It's about evidence and facts."

Fleming pushed his plate away. "Unlike this murder, where we still don't know who did the crime." Fleming brightened and said, "I happen to have a few facts for you to consider."

Lundin could tell from Fleming's enthusiasm that he had more than a few facts. He took out his notebook. "Let's get started."

Fleming raised his hand for the waitress. "Another bourbon please, and for my friend ...?"

"Coffee, please."

Fleming shook his head and turned to the waitress. "Two coffees and another bourbon, please."

When the drinks arrived at the table, Fleming began his report.

"While you were interviewing Stevens, I sent a request to Room 39. I had previously called them to let them know it was coming. I may have a slow fist when it comes to Morse code, but even so, it was a bit annoying sending and receiving the material."

Lundin nodded. He had no experience with wireless communications, but it certainly had looked difficult when he watched the telegraphers at rail stations sending his messages from the Northwest Territories to RCMP offices in Edmonton or Winnipeg. "I suppose it isn't as if you can send a detailed tasking or receive a detailed report."

Fleming shook his head. "I'm sure you have sent telegrams in the past, so you know you must consider brevity. What I asked for was information on Novosel and whether there was anyone in the camp who had a connection to SOE in Yugoslavia. I figured that given our victim and Novosel were both Serbs, that was a good start."

Lundin hadn't considered a military connection to Yugoslavia. Instead, he had wondered about some Canadian link to the Yugoslavian community. For the first time, he realized that Fleming was really going to be a useful partner rather than an amusing colleague. He said, "I hadn't thought of a wartime connection."

"That is one of the interesting pieces. But first, here's what we know about Novosel. He was recruited early on to serve as a translator for SOE teams going into Yugoslavia. He wasn't in the military at that point, they just approached him directly." He paused to work on his bourbon. "I know from experience that the SOE uses several different connections to get the people they need. University professors are their real talent spotters, but for language skills they use any means possible to make a connection. In 1939, Novosel was working as a machinist in the Hawker factory, making Hurricanes. Hard work and long hours. I'm sure when the SOE approached him, the idea of a new job must have been appealing."

"So Novosel isn't a commando?"

"That comes later. Apparently, he went out as a translator in an early SOE team working with the Royalists in Serbia. They are known as the Chetniks, and their leader is a senior member of the Yugoslavian army. The SOE call their teams lots of different names, but often they simply use women's names. His team was called MAINSTREAM. All I know from the telegram is MAINSTREAM didn't go well and Novosel barely got out alive. When he returned to England, he joined the Commandos and served on the St. Nazaire raid."

"The connection with Novak."

"Exactly. Like many of the Commandos, he was on the Campbeltown. And, like Novak, he was one of the few who made it back. He was wounded in action and has been recuperating in a hospital in Scotland. That's all Room 39 had for me today. They promised more if they could find more, but I reckon that was most useful."

"Interesting to be sure, but useful for our investigation? Ian, I'm not following you."

"Well, the second piece of information might help close the loop.

Room 39 reported that one of the instructors here was in Yugoslavia. And, he was the team leader for MAINSTREAM."

Lundin could see that Fleming was enjoying this bit of intrigue, having planned the revelations precisely to maximize the suspense. He said, "OK, Ian. If you are going to make me ask, I will ask. Who?"

"The commander for MAINSTREAM was Hamish Creed."

"Well, isn't that interesting?"

"Indeed. An odd little coincidence, don't you think?"

"I don't believe in coincidences, Ian. Connections like this make me very curious. We will have to see what happens tomorrow when I ask the good major why he didn't point out he had a connection to Yugoslavia."

"I suspect there will be more from Room 39 tomorrow."

Lundin decided to deliver his own bit of suspense. "Before dinner, I called Toronto. I briefed the chief inspector on today's results and asked him to task the archivist to find out everything we have on Ken Stevens. There is something incomplete about the way he tells the story of Novak. I'm not saying he is involved in the murder, but he is hiding something. Perhaps RCMP Montreal knows what that is."

"Montreal?"

"Stevens was a professor at McGill University before the war. If he has any skeletons in his closet from those years, it just might explain my feeling."

Fleming raised his glass in a toast. "To those who keep the records. We never know what they might find."

Lundin nodded. "Evidence is what we want, Ian. Perhaps evidence is what they will deliver."

Fleming smiled. "Would gossip do?"

Lundin said, "Gossip might just do."

"While I was in HYDRA, I asked one of the operators how things were with Stevens and Novak. He said they seemed close."

"Just as Stevens said."

"But recently Stevens has been out of sorts. Do you want to know why?"

"Because his friend is dead?"

"As I said, sarcasm is not your best game. No, because Stevens said he lost his lucky silver dollar. He made the operators tear apart their desks looking for a silver dollar. None of the operators are amused."

"Isn't that interesting?"

Fleming took another sip of his drink. "I thought so."

The Investigation: Day Four
Images in the Fog

17 October 1942, Oshawa

CHAPTER FIFTEEN — THE RCMP FILES

Lundin came down to the hotel restaurant well before dawn. He had spent a restless night thinking about the case and finally just gave up, washed, shaved, polished his boots, donned his uniform and walked down the stairs. The simple effort to get back into a proper uniform helped improve his disposition. He needed coffee, ideally an entire pot.

The restaurant staff arrived a half hour later to find their Mountie, as they had started to call him, already at a table set for four. He had moved the place settings away and was working on some sort of project using his notebook and a small pencil. The waitress came up to see if she could help. Lundin looked up and said, "Coffee, please. Black and lots of it."

She nodded and walked away. She said to her husband, who was the morning cook, "Our Mountie looks like he has been up all night."

"Charlotte, that's an easy order. There is a note from the night staff saying that our Navy officer stayed up half the night drinking. I don't expect him anytime soon. What does our Mountie want for breakfast?"

"For now, just coffee."

The cook nodded and returned to his work setting up the kitchen for requests for eggs, bacon, home-fried potatoes and pancakes. He started mixing batter for the morning muffins and wondered what was keeping the Mountie up all night. Was it the murder on the shoreline? The cook had heard from workers at the camp that they had found a body in the lake. The dead man must have been mighty important for a Mountie to take charge. The cook's thoughts wandered as he mixed the batter. Finally, he walked over to the waitress and said, "Do you think our Mountie would like to hear from Neal, the cook from the camp? I think he might be able to help."

"I will ask, but only after he has had a couple of cups. He looks like a man who might be plenty grumpy in the morning."

"Unlike me, eh?"

Charlotte threw a bar towel at her husband. "I'm not going to answer that."

Lundin was grumpy, for sure. There were too many moving parts to this story and too few bits of evidence to pull them all together. He needed something and he needed it soon. From his experience, the longer an investigation took the less likely that the investigation would succeed. He was not about to return to Toronto to report that he had failed in this sensitive investigation.

He drew two diagrams in his notebook. First, there was the Yugoslav link. Novak was found in the water by a Yugoslav student and Fleming. He was in contact with another Yugoslavian named Novosel who he met earlier this year. And, Lundin's Camp X focal point, Hamish Creed was an SOE officer who served in Yugoslavia at the beginning of the war. Surely that must be a main investigative thread.

On another page, there was a smaller diagram. Novak was the night supervisor for a very sensitive communications facility. His supervisor, Stevens, had nothing but praise for his performance. But there was the mysterious coin found in his shoe. And Stevens had lost a coin, possibly the same one. It looked like something out of a spy novel from the 1930s. Something that the governor general might have dreamed up during the war when he wrote the Richard Hanney novels. Espionage was a possibility, but he couldn't figure out how it fit into his murder case. He said to himself, "Well, Lundin, you wanted an important case. Don't moan about it."

The waitress cleared her throat. She had approached the table quietly holding the coffee pot. Lundin was embarrassed that she had heard his comment. He realized he was talking to himself and that wasn't a good sign. He raised his mug, and as she filled it he said, "It's been a long night."

"Sir, my husband Ralph wondered if you would have time to talk to our friend Neal. He is the cook at the camp. Ralph thinks Neal might have something worthwhile to say."

Lundin brightened. On the one hand, he knew that his countrymen would often offer help simply as part of their natural Canadian friendliness, or because a crime investigation could add a bit of excitement in an otherwise mundane daily life. Still, in at least one of his cases in Winnipeg, a volunteer had provided an eyewitness account that closed an equally challenging murder investigation. He said, "I would like that very much. Do you think Neal would prefer to meet at the camp or here?"

"Sir, I know he would like to meet here. He said they work him ever so hard at the camp and they are always looking over his shoulder. They are a real hush-hush outfit at the camp."

"Tonight? I would be happy to buy him a beer if he would take the time to see me. Just name the time."

"Neal usually comes over after five. Our shift is done and his is as well. Neal and Ralph are mates. They share a beer before he goes home to his wife and kids."

"Shall we make it six, then?"

"I will check with Ralph and get back to you before breakfast service is over. Would you like something other than coffee now?"

A voice came from the entrance to the dining room. "He would and so would I, ma'am. I am famished!"

Lundin smiled and shook his head. He looked up at the waitress. "Let's have two full breakfasts and more coffee."

Charlotte went back to the kitchen and told her husband the news. He said, "I will make sure Neal is ready to talk to our Mountie. Meanwhile, I need to get started on their breakfasts. It's a good thing they are early risers. There are three more guests for breakfast today. They booked a breakfast at nine. Can you believe it? They *booked* a breakfast. As if we were the Ritz. They must be from New York. No one ever books breakfast except New Yorkers."

Ralph turned back to his stoves and started the burners. "Two full breakfasts it will be!"

"Miles, have you decided how we should proceed? When are we going to confront Creed? I would very much like to be there."

Lundin suspected Creed was one of several instructors who were especially harsh on Fleming while he was in training. "Ian, the secret to a good interview is to know as much as possible before you start."

"Our interrogators in the London Cage have told me the same."

"London Cage?"

"Apologies for the descriptive term. When I first heard that we were interviewing POWs in what was called the London Cage, I thought to myself that even for Axis POWs that would be a bit harsh." The coffees arrived and Fleming paused to take a sip from the white ceramic mug. "It is just what the Army intelligence chaps call any interrogation facility. It is certainly a controlled facility, but neither a cage nor, to be honest, a prison. It is a building in central London where senior POWs are encouraged to tell more than their name, their rank and service number. Our interrogators have terrific language skills and spend hours preparing for their first interview. They said to me that their first interview is designed to make sure the POW knows that we know more about them than they know themselves. The Double Cross team told me the same thing."

"Another British military code name?"

"It is a joint military, Secret Service and Security Service team called the Twenty Committee. It's called the Double Cross because they use Roman numerals — two Xs — for their paperwork."

Lundin shook his head. He wondered if the British spent as much time actually fighting the war as they did coming up with whimsical names for their operations. In the Great War, his regiment fell under the command of a British Army Corps. Periodically, he delivered messages to the British staff. He found them far too jocular for trench life. He said, "How cute."

"Fair enough, Miles. You must remember that most of our seniors come from a small number of British public schools — confusing, since you call them private schools — and the public school system teaches dead languages, English poetry and eccentricities like word-play with puns and anagrams. I suppose it is just a part of our heritage."

"And you?"

"Oh, never fear, I am an old Etonian. More or less. I was good at sports, moderately good in classes, but a troublemaker who was asked to leave a little early."

"Somehow, I'm not surprised."

"Well, it wasn't all my fault."

"Ian, I can't tell you how many times a villain has said that to me."

Fleming laughed out loud. "Before you start your interrogation of my dreary youth, what are you going to do about Creed?"

"I haven't decided yet. He certainly has the skills, and there is something in the way of a motive buried in his SOE past. I just need some sort of hook to use for the next time I see him."

"Angler, are you?"

Lundin was slowly getting used to Fleming jumping back and forth between subjects. Before he could think of something clever to say, their meals arrived. Once the waitress was gone and Fleming had a mouth full of pancakes and sausage, he said, "Yes. When there is time. Both lake and stream. I am Canadian, and that means hunting and fishing is part of who I am." Before he took his first bite, he nodded toward the waitress as she walked away. "It seems we have a new witness on the horizon. Our waitress and her husband are pals with the chief cook at the camp. He wants to talk to me tonight. Says he saw something the night of the murder."

Fleming put his fork down. "Did he indeed!"

"Ian, don't get your hopes up. Canadians are always willing to help the Mounties."

"Except when they aren't."

"Well, that's usually because they are villains. Anyway, I have found that eyewitness accounts don't always clarify. They sometimes add to the fog of an investigation. We will just have to wait and see. I will be fortifying our witness with a pint tonight."

"Excellent. Have you heard back from Montreal?"

Lundin looked at his watch. "It's a bit early yet. I will call after breakfast."

Fleming waved to the waitress for more coffee. He said, "Have you noticed we are the only people in the dining room?"

"It is also just 6 a.m., Ian. Who else goes to a hotel and gets up before dawn?"

"Fair point." The waitress poured the coffee and returned to the kitchen. "What is the plan for today?"

"It will depend on what I hear from my people. I'm hoping for something, honestly anything, about our Canadians. It might not be something that pushes our case forward, but if it gives me a wedge to use against one of them, that might be enough."

"Who are your subjects?"

"I wanted more on Ken Stevens. Professors almost always have something odd in their history. Otherwise, they wouldn't be professors."

Fleming smirked at him, and Lundin clarified, "OK. I will admit I'm a little prejudiced against the ivory towers. I made it through high school and then went off to war. After the war, I joined the Force. I've had plenty of training, but nothing you might call advanced education."

"Nor I, unless you count my days at Sandhurst."

"The military college? You had an Army career first?"

"No, Miles. Another false start in my rather eccentric resume."

Lundin could see that this was as much on the subject as he was going to get from Fleming. He continued, "I also want to see if there might be something about your mate Jovanovic, as well as Flight Lieutenant Beatrice Thomas."

"When it comes to Jovanovic, I can vouch for the man. He was with me the whole time on the exercise and, in any event, he is one of those salt-of-the-earth types."

"Plenty of those types of men murder other salts of the earth."

"I will take your word for that. As to Beatrice, she has the soul of an adventurer. I thought we might be more compatible than we are…"

"As in, you thought you might become *closer* to the lieutenant."

"You can't blame me for trying. She is good-looking and far more outgoing than the three other women in the class. The other three are destined to be radio operators while Thomas is far more likely to be an agent in the field." Fleming paused over his hash-brown potatoes. "Do you always use onions with your potatoes?"

"Only at breakfast."

"Hmmm. Well, I think I will stick with my eggs and bacon." As he used his knife to cut his bacon, Fleming said, "Did you know that Thomas was an ambulance driver in Spain? She returned to Canada and became a pilot. Delivered fighters and bombers across the Atlantic. Amazing."

Lundin stopped eating and made a notation in his notebook. He wrote: *Thomas, Spain.* "Ian, that is the sort of information I need. Anything on your salt of the earth?"

"Jovanovic worked your ore freighters before the war. A machinist mate. He joined the Navy and did the same duty in the Canadian Navy. He said to me that he wanted to get out of the belly of a ship and back to Yugoslavia to fight the Nazis. I couldn't blame him."

"He said that same thing to me. If he was in freighters before the war, he was probably a union man like Novak. He claimed not to know him."

"A fair distance between a wireless operator and the man running the boilers, eh?"

"True enough. But the unions tend to split into like-minded and sometimes ethnic groups. Still, it's a long stretch if they weren't in the same union hall."

Fleming looked over at Lundin's plate. "You are the one not eating this morning."

"Too busy thinking, Ian."

"I'll stop questioning and let you eat. We need to get back to work at the camp."

CHAPTER SIXTEEN — A FILE ON A PROFESSOR AND THE INCOMPLETE HISTORY OF TEAM MAINSTREAM

As they drove toward Camp X, Lundin shared what he had learned over the phone. "We don't really keep files on Canadians unless they have a criminal record. Still, if a citizen has some sort of legal problem with the national or provincial government, we can recover it. And, since we entered the war, other parts of the government have been helpful as well."

"A good prologue, Miles. But, as newspapermen say, stop burying the lede."

"It turns out that our professor has an interesting background. He was part of the war industry in the Great War. Plenty of work building wireless communications for the Canadian Navy. He did have a bit of trouble with the local authorities in Quebec when he tried to unionize the workforce during the war. Asking for better wages and fewer hours is not something you do in the middle of a war."

"Unless you are a Bolshie."

"Indeed, unless you are Bolshevik. So, Stevens suddenly is listed in a police file as an agitator. Never charged, but put on a watch list. As we go into the early twenties, when just about everyone in the US and England are convinced that any industrial action is part of some red conspiracy, a separate RCMP investigation uncovers Stevens' membership card with the Wobblies."

"Miles, you just made that up."

"Sorry, the Industrial Workers of the World. It was a union started in Chicago before the war but expanded after the war. Whether true or not, in the twenties it was considered a Bolshevik front. For certain, the Wobblies were affiliated with anarchists, socialists and some Bolsheviks. In the US the Wobblies demonstrated against the war, and the Canadian government banned the organization during the war."

"That doesn't sound like the Stevens we met."

"No, it doesn't." Lundin smiled and said, "But it does give me something to talk about, eh?"

"The fact that a Bolshie, or as you say, a Wobbly, is now managing the engineering at a secret communications site? Now, I know the Soviets are our allies against the Nazis, but it certainly looks curious."

"Yes, indeed."

"Any other tidbits?"

"Well, as you said, our records confirm the flight lieutenant was in Spain during their civil war. We don't know much about her time there, other than her passport information. I'm assuming she was involved with the Republicans rather than Franco's bunch, but that's just speculation on my part since she has been working against the Nazis since 1939. Further grist for my mill."

"I will have to tell you sometime about my trip to Spain."

"Not an anarchist, are you?"

"Heaven forbid! Do I look like someone who has any interest in political philosophy?"

"Only with regard to defeating the Nazis — or if a woman was involved."

"I'll give you that comment. So, what else do we know about Thomas?"

"That's where it gets odd. There are no records, no records at all, for Thomas before she returned to Canada. There isn't even a passport application. We know she came back from Spain in 1937. Passport records show Thomas on a Canadian passport arriving in Halifax. The next federal document is her pilot's license in 1938."

"Does she come from a wealthy family? I mean, after all, how do you get the money to travel to Spain and then take flight lessons? How do you eat?"

"One of the questions that I intend to pose when I get a chance to interview her."

"Good luck. I suspect she is in the final problem exercise at the camp. We might not be able to see her or Jovanovic until the weekend. And, we need to be sure we see them before they are shipped off to England. They should be loaded on an aircraft by early next week."

"Then we had better have some success today. Are you expecting more information from your people?"

"The communicator for Room 39 told me yesterday that he would be transmitting at 0930hrs local." He looked at his Rolex and said, "We have about an hour before I need to be inside HYDRA."

"That should be plenty of time, unless the gate guards are a problem."

"Leave that to me, Miles."

As Fleming promised, there were no challenges at the main gate or, for that matter, at the entrance to HYDRA. Fleming shooed away the staff as if he owned the place and walked toward the communications room. Lundin was constantly amazed that Fleming could simply breeze through the administrative challenges at Camp X. All his life, Lundin had obeyed the rules and stayed inside the boundaries of the law. He suspected that was the difference between a man born of wealth and a man born from the working classes. When you had been poor, you wanted to keep working because you wanted to keep eating. To keep working, you followed the rules. He ended his musings as Stevens walked up.

The man looked harried. His bowtie was unknotted, his rolled-up shirtsleeves were uneven and part of his shirt tail was creeping out from his trousers. He said, "Sergeant Lundin, I had not expected to see you today."

Lundin responded to his formality. "Is this a bad time, Mr. Stevens?"

"I'm dealing with some sort of problem with one of the antennas, and my night shift supervisor — the one who replaced Ned — came down sick. As a Canadian, you know that we are headed into the season of colds and fevers. I'm hoping we don't have a small epidemic on our hands like I saw right after the war."

Lundin needed Stevens to calm down and see his upcoming questions in the most positive light possible. "Well do I remember the Spanish flu. I hadn't been demobbed from my regiment and half my platoon came down with the flu. Of those, only about five survived. It was terrifying."

"I didn't see the crisis until after I finished my time in the factories. I was in school finishing my degree when the flu hit Montreal. They closed the schools. I worked for a bit at a small company making electric motors for generators. All of us came down with the flu. The union kept us on the payroll even though the managers didn't see why we should be paid since we weren't doing our jobs."

"It was a tough time in Canada in the twenties."

"Tough for some, fantastic for others. Factory owners could offer any pay they chose because folks needed work. It really wasn't until the crash that there was some leveling of the pain."

"So, when did you get back to school?"

"McGill reopened in '25 and I finished my degrees in '33. They offered me a teaching job and I grabbed it with both hands. It was in the middle of the Depression. It wasn't as if industry was going to hire any new electrical engineers."

"Ken, I apologize for waiting this long to ask: are you married? Do you have children?"

Stevens shook his head. The sweat on his brow had made what little hair he had stand up; the head shake only made his face seem more ridiculous. For a moment, Lundin felt sorry for the man. He said, "Shall we stop and get a cup of tea? Perhaps take our mugs of tea outside?"

"We don't allow any beverages near the wireless sets or the other electronics. Too dangerous for the tubes and the wiring. We have a small canteen in the back. I think a cup of tea would be most helpful."

They walked past racks of communication equipment that hummed slightly as the electricity ran through the tubes and wires. There didn't appear to be much in the way of insulation around the machinery. Lundin steered well clear of the racks. He didn't know much about electronics, but he had worked accident scenes around high-power wires and electricity. The only thing he knew for certain was electricity could kill. Stevens appeared unaware of Lundin's concern and offered a lecture on the equipment as they walked along the racks and between workstations where men were studiously watching gauges and adjusting dials. None of it made sense to Lundin, but he had learned years ago that so long as he nodded and occasionally added a comment like, "I see," the lecturer would simply believe he understood or, at least, cared about the topic.

The canteen was little more than a closet with a small stove, a copper kettle, multiple poorly washed white ceramic mugs and a tall can with teabags. Lundin thought a good cleaning from top to bottom might be a decent start to avoid disease, but he kept the idea to himself. However, when they did finally get water to boil, he filled his cup twice: once to sterilize the grime, and then a second time for his tea. He took his tea black because the sugar bowl seemed to be filled with black speckles. He could only imagine what they might be. Stevens took his tea with milk from a small aluminum pitcher and then shoveled three spoons of sugar into the mug. He stirred the tea with the spoon and then pushed it back into the sugar bowl. Lundin was ready to step outside at that point even if the weather would remind him that mid-October in Ontario was just one step away from winter. As they walked out the back door of the canteen, the wind cut through Lundin's wool tunic. He realized that he should have brought an overcoat when he left Toronto.

Stevens seemed unaffected. "It is so good to be outside." He pointed to one of the far antennas. There were two men on a scaffold working on the guy-wires. "They are almost done. We had to take down the antenna, reattach the wires connecting it to HYDRA and then put the antenna back up. At least that will be something accomplished today."

Lundin could feel that Stevens was becoming comfortable with the conversation, perhaps dropping his guard as he found a sympathetic ear from the Mountie. Sympathetic or not, Lundin perceived it was time to gently probe the ex-professor's background. He said, "The factory work during the war had to be at least as hard as this one, no?"

"Hard in a different way, Sergeant. We had a job to do for the war effort. Everyone was committed to the cause. Of course, that didn't stop the bosses from profiting from the war."

Stevens stopped talking for a moment as he sipped his tea. Lundin knew that sometimes the best weapon in an interrogation was silence. After nearly a minute, Stevens continued. "Here we are helping to fight the Nazis and the Fascists. Back in the last war, they wanted to put us all under their thumb. At the end, they even had the temerity to attack the Soviet Union. Can you imagine how mad that is? Today, it is the greatest industrial power on the planet. Back in the first war, we were fighting for the Crown. But did the Germans and the Austrians and the Turks really threaten us the way the Nazis threaten us? I wonder."

Lundin had to force himself not to argue the point about the Soviet Union's great industrial power. He suspected workers in Canada and the US would see things differently. Still, it opened a small door and he intended to walk through the door to see what was on the other side. "Have you been to Germany or the Soviet Union? I am a Canadian, with no experience of anyplace other than North America except my time in the Great War."

The college professor came to the surface. He might have been in a lecture hall at McGill rather than a cold windy day on the shore of Lake Ontario. "I did visit both countries in the late thirties. The Nazis and the Soviets both understand how to mobilize their people. Both are industrial giants. And, while I think the Nazi philosophy is hateful, they were taking greater care of their people than we are in Canada or the Americans are down south. In the Soviet Union, the philosophy is focused entirely on the people — and the results are easy to see. Big factories, excellent education, housing for the people, and no one goes hungry. They call it a workers' paradise. That's all bluster, of course, but they are working toward that goal. I suppose that's why Hitler had to attack them. They threatened his entire political philosophy. In the Soviet Union, the people are the government. In Germany, Hitler is the government."

Lundin now could see Stevens as a Wobbly. He wasn't about to throw bombs, but he certainly was committed to what the Reds were doing in the USSR and, perhaps, what they were trying to do elsewhere. No wonder the Force had a file on the man. The good news was he didn't hide in the shadows. At least not until he moved to Camp X. That gave Lundin an idea. "Are you working both shifts tonight?" he asked. "When will you sleep?"

Stevens nodded. "I will work through midnight, and then one of my day-shift supervisors will spare me. It isn't ideal, but it is about all we can do until the Army or the Navy provide us with another senior radioman." He looked up at Lundin and said, "By the way, what did you come here to ask me?"

Lundin had prepared for the question and responded, "I wondered if you had any other information about Novak's time in the Navy. You said he was a good wireless operator. I wondered if you knew anything more about his time at sea? You said he didn't have any friends in the camp. It must be pretty lonely working night shift and not being able to tell family what you are doing for the war."

"Ned never talked about his family. I got the impression both parents were dead, but that is about all I know. I told you about his Navy time and his time with the Commandos. He was very quiet about the early war years. As to contacts in camp or in town, I don't know of any friends. He worked nights and slept days. I used to see him walking along the beach and sometimes around the antenna field, but otherwise he just kept to himself."

Lundin nodded. One part of a good interrogation was to revisit the same ground to see if the subject's story remained consistent. Stevens' response had passed that test, at least about Novak's life outside work. There was still something that he wasn't talking about, something related to Stevens' guilt over Novak's death. If Novak was just a colleague who worked the other half of the clock, why did Stevens argue against the easy answer the rest of the camp wanted? It would have been much easier to simply accept Novak's death as an accident. Lundin hoped that the plan he was hatching in his head would answer that question, ideally tonight. He said, "Ken, thanks for your time. I know you are busy and I will let you get back to your work. I promise to let you know if I find any answers on Novak's death."

"Thank you, Sergeant." With that, Stevens turned and walked quickly back to the canteen. Lundin wondered if he was relieved or just cold. As he walked more slowly back to the rear door of HYDRA, one of the guards approached.

"Sergeant, I'll take the mug inside for you. You can return to your car, if you please."

Lundin sighed. The bureaucracy of secrecy was closing the door on him. He nodded and passed the mug to the military policeman. "Thank you, Private."

"You're welcome, Sergeant. Have a good day."

Lundin worked through the results of this recent conversation as he walked to the Buick. His thoughts were interrupted as he heard a voice call his name. He looked around to see Hamish Creed jogging across the parade ground. Creed was dressed in a camouflage field jacket top, brown wool trousers and military boots. He waved and said, "Miles, what luck to see you."

Lundin thought for a moment about whether this meeting was luck or planning on Creed's part. Either way, it didn't look like he could avoid the conversation. He shouted, "Hamish, good to see you. I thought for certain you would be too busy with your students. I didn't want to waste your time as I worked through the details of Novak's death."

Creed walked the last few yards, closing to just a few feet before he spoke again. "Thanks for that. We are now in the final problem, and that means long hours testing the students in every one of the skills they have learned over the past three weeks. We have already eliminated all the dead weight, so this is more about teaching them how to integrate their skills rather than evaluating the students. Only about 48 more hours. Then we hold an informal passing out parade and send them by train to Kingston, where they are dispatched from the RCAF Air Station to Britain."

"A job well done, then. When does the next class begin?"

"I suspect not until the SOE talent spotters are done. Probably just after Christmas. I will be traveling back to Britain with the students. They will be going onward to the SOE training center in Beaulieu. It looks like my exile to Canada is over."

"And then back to Europe?" Creed looked uncomfortable. Lundin wasn't sure if it was because he didn't want to reveal some secret plan or because he wasn't sure how to answer. Lundin added, "Of course, if it is a military secret, then I really don't need to know. I was just curious."

Creed flushed slightly. "Miles, I don't suppose it reveals any state secrets that I will probably be a dispatcher for a time. That means I will make sure our SOE teams end up with the right kit, the right mission and loaded on the right aircraft or Royal Navy craft. I don't know if my action days are over, or simply delayed until they find a suitable mission."

Lundin decided to probe just a bit. "Are you a French speaker, then?"

Creed nodded. "Passable French. I'm better in Greek."

"So, the Adriatic."

"When the time is right."

"You said you were deployed before coming here. Was it in Greece then?"

"Actually, it was Yugoslavia. A dark place to be sure. Plenty of intrigues among the various groups, and Serbo-Croatian is impenetrable."

"I suppose some of the resistance folks speak English or Greek."

"Some do. As I said when we first met, that's one of the reasons why we are searching for native speakers here in Canada. Jovanovic for example will be a great resource for a team in Yugoslavia."

"He made the cut and is headed to England?"

"Oh, yes. He is a sturdy chap. I was wondering how the investigation is going?"

"Hamish, like so many of my investigations, it goes in fits and starts. After all, your camp medical team made it clear that this was an accident. We call it a suspicious death because we must do so. After all, no one saw Novak fall into the water. It's just something that must be accomplished."

Lundin watched Creed as he told the lie. Creed initially looked worried, then relieved as he presented the investigation as a simple bureaucratic process to close the file. Creed said, "Well then, it shouldn't take you too much longer."

"For goodness sake, Hamish. This is only day four of the investigation. I would like to be finished by tomorrow. If the report isn't complete, the chief inspector will send me back to finish the job. As I said, it is a bureaucratic process." Lundin offered his most friendly of smiles which, if he was honest, often looked more like a snarl than a smile. Still, it seemed to relieve Creed's worries. And that was precisely what he wanted. As Creed relaxed and turned to leave, Lundin returned to the topic of Yugoslavia. "You said you barely made it out of Yugoslavia last time. Did you talk about that with Jovanovic so that he knows how dangerous it can be?"

The question stopped Creed in his tracks. He turned back to Lundin. "He grew up in that country. He knows all about the challenges of feuding warlords and local religious hatreds. I was the outsider last time, and I certainly am not about to lecture him on his own country."

"When you mentioned it before, I thought you were talking about the Nazis. Now are you saying it was locals who were the threat?"

"Both. These folks see the Nazis as occupiers, but they also have utility in eliminating their local rivals. That means sometimes they fight the Nazis and sometimes they collaborate with the Nazis. As an outsider, it was hard to tell friend from foe."

Lundin decided he had pulled on the string as hard as he could. He would come back to this story, if necessary, but he didn't want Creed to suspect anything. Still, he would have to move quickly if Creed was headed back to the UK in a few days. He said, "Hamish, that sounds like my time up in the Northwest Territories. Miners, tribal folk and small businessmen. Sometimes allies, sometimes adversaries — and I was caught in the middle."

Creed nodded. "Exactly, Miles. Now, I must return to the training. I hope to see you again before I leave."

Lundin waved. "Count on it, Hamish."

As Lundin turned toward the Buick, he saw Fleming leaning against the car. "Lurking, Ian?"

"Eavesdropping has been a habit for years. You never know when you might hear something useful."

"One of a small number of your faults."

"Consider it survival instinct. I thought you handled Creed perfectly. You got him to talk about MAINSTREAM without making him suspicious. He isn't much of a spy, is he?"

"Well, I'm not sure that many of the SOE types are spies. Creed made it clear when we first talked that they were more like commandos who worked with the locals. But you are right. I hope he isn't a card player. He doesn't hide his feelings all that well. I know of poker players who would take him to the cleaners."

"Few play poker in Britain. But he wouldn't be much of a bridge partner."

"Too complicated a game for me."

"And it requires working with a partner. I suspect that's something you would find annoying."

"Do I look annoyed with you?"

"Most of the time, Miles. Most of the time!"

Lundin raised his hands in mock surrender. "Are we done here?"

"I'm done with HYDRA and ready for a drink."

Lundin looked at his watch. It was 4 p.m. He said, "I recommend we go back to the hotel. We have an appointment with an eyewitness and then…well, I have something I want to do tonight, and a clear head is going to be required."

Fleming rubbed his hands. "Night work? Excellent!"

For once, Fleming was quiet on their drive to the hotel. When they arrived, Lundin said, "Ian, why don't we meet in the bar at five. We can review our notes of the day and then meet with our eyewitness. After that, dinner and our night work. If you have some outdoor kit available, please wear it."

Fleming nodded and headed to his room. When he came back down to the bar at five, he found Lundin dressed entirely in navy-blue wool including heavy trousers, a sweater and a pair of black work boots. He said, "I didn't realize we needed commando kit for tonight."

Lundin looked at Fleming's wardrobe. His outfit might have been better suited for an afternoon of fly fishing. His clothes were a mix of tweed and gabardine. "There is something that I want to do at the camp. I intend to arrive by canoe. I have heard you know a bit about that sort of thing."

Fleming nodded. "Indeed I do. I hope I won't be expected to swim as well as paddle."

"Let's hope not."

"I'll go upstairs and change to something more suitable. Be back in a tick." When Fleming returned, he was wearing forest-green wool pants and his wool roll neck, and was carrying his leather flight jacket.

Lundin nodded. "Much better." Lundin pointed to his coffee mug. "We have some time if you want to get a coffee and tell me the latest from Room 39. Then I will relate my activities this morning."

Fleming returned to the table with a mug of coffee and a glass of bourbon. Lundin shook his head. "Ian, I need you to have a clear head tonight."

"Just this one, I promise. Now, before you hear the epistle from Room 39, tell me how your conversations with Stevens and Creed went."

"Stevens revealed a bit about his support for socialism, and even offered a full-throated support to the 'workers' paradise' known as the USSR."

"I would not have thought anyone still would think Joseph Stalin's world was a paradise."

"Nor I. But remember, I am a mere servant of the Crown."

Fleming replied with a full dose of sarcasm, "Just as I am merely a personal aide to a Royal Navy admiral."

"I think there is far more to Mr. Stevens than meets the eye. I intend to visit his room tonight while he is working his split shift at HYDRA."

"A bit of burglary? By a Mountie?"

"Let's just remember that Camp X is Canadian military property and no one in the camp should expect a degree of privacy."

"And you need me to protect your back."

"Exactly. Stevens said his room was next to Novak's. That means it should be relatively easy to get in and out. And if Stevens was the one who stole Novak's papers — or anything else for that matter — we should be able to find them."

"And you told me that there wasn't going to be anything like fictional adventures."

"I think I said there were very few adventures."

"And what did Creed have to say for himself?"

Lundin related the conversation. At the end, he said, "Did Room 39 have any additional information?"

Fleming looked at his empty bourbon glass, then at Lundin, who shook his head. He took a sip from his coffee and said, "Well, Room 39 had some interesting stories to tell. First, Team MAINSTREAM was an early team into Yugoslavia. Less than a year after SOE was founded. The teams at that point had far less training than they do now. Creed came from the Commandos. They had a rigorous selection program and Creed passed with flying colours. He was about to be transferred to North Africa with No. 7 Commando when someone in SOE found out that Creed spoke Greek. They grabbed him from his unit and sent him to Cairo. The plan was to have him inserted into Greece or Crete, but at the last minute they needed an officer to engage the resistance in Montenegro. They matched Creed up with Novosel and sent them in by submarine to the coast. There was no reception committee…"

"Sorry, Ian. A reception committee?"

"Just like it sounds. A friendly group waiting for you at a dropping zone or a beach who will then take you to a resistance headquarters."

"No reception committee for MAINSTREAM."

"As I said, it was early days in this underground warfare effort. Heaven only knows how SOE Cairo thought they would proceed, but Creed was game. Novosel wasn't thrilled, but he was from Montenegro so he thought it would be possible to meet with someone who might help them."

"Not a bet I would make."

"Nor I. I far prefer working with an assault force of commandos. But, that was the mission and Creed and Novosel accepted the risks. Novosel was successful at first. He found a relative who was willing to introduce them to a local who was part of a resistance cell. They followed the line up what we might call the chain of command, though it was probably more like a gathering of bandits. Again, remember, I was getting a telegram-style message. I'm not going to give you many details."

"Fair enough, Ian. What was the result?"

"MAINSTREAM was compromised by one of Novosel's relatives. Creed was able to escape, but only because he left Novosel behind. He made it to the shoreline and waited for a scheduled supply drop. They didn't even have a radio with them, poor sods. Creed makes it back to Cairo. Novosel escapes somehow. He gets a family member to take him to a Greek island and then gets back to Cairo. He denounces Creed. There is an investigation. Creed is exonerated but sent to SOE

Headquarters and eventually to Camp X. Novosel recovers in a Cairo hospital. He joins the Commandos and is sent back to Britain for training. The poor bastard then gets selected for another unconventional mission — St. Nazaire. He survives. Is wounded again and is back in Britain recuperating. He is currently assigned to No. 10 Commando, which is made up of foreigners in Britain. Heaven only knows what mission they will be given."

"It starts to make sense why Novosel was writing to Novak and why the Bible passage on revenge."

"Are you saying Creed could be our murderer?"

"I've known men who have murdered for less. Sometimes a dark past is something you will do anything to keep in the past."

"I found Creed to be a pill, but I can't imagine him as the murderer."

"He just became a suspect. That doesn't mean he will be the murderer. And, remember what I said yesterday. We need evidence. There are plenty of men in Canada who might want me dead, but few would be able or willing to make that happen."

"Could it be Stevens?"

"I think not. But I'm not going to rule out the possibility that he and Novak had a disagreement that ended in violence."

"And then there is our treasure map."

"Indeed. That sounds more like a spy story than a murder."

"Spies do kill people. After all, that's what Camp X teaches. They lecture that in this war, there are no rules and, if you are trapped, it is kill or be killed. Finally, if you find a traitor, you need to eliminate them…permanently."

Lundin thought for a moment that all of those teaching points could have applied as well to his time in the trenches in France. As to traitors, he would want to prove they were traitors before they were hanged. He looked at his watch. It was nearly 6 p.m. He said, "Time to meet our eyewitness."

CHAPTER SEVENTEEN — NIGHT WORK

They walked into the kitchen to find Neal flanked by his two friends from the hotel. Lundin would have guessed Neal was in his early 50s. He looked much like the hunting camp cooks he met in the Northwest Territories: a little over five feet tall and painfully thin. Lundin always wondered why cooks were either a full axe-handle wide or pencil thin. Neal was dressed in dungarees, a t-shirt and a hunter's plaid coat. Rubber boots completed his trousseau. He had a week's growth of beard and grey hair that barely made it above his ears before retreating to a bald spot. An ancient-looking pipe pulled to one side of his mouth offered a foul-smelling vapor of cheap tobacco. Lundin wondered how good a cook he might be. Fleming answered the question as he walked forward and shook the man's hand.

"Sir, I understand you are the head chef at the camp. I want you to know that I have had more than my share of military meals and yours have been the best."

Neal stood up straight and brightened. Lundin could have sworn he grew four inches with the complement. He spoke around the pipe stem, "Glad to hear that, your honor. Glad to hear it."

Lundin stepped closer and said, "Neal, I'm Miles Lundin from the Mounties. I'm mighty glad you were willing to talk to us."

The cook nodded and said, "Sergeant, I'm Neal Dixon. I served in the Forces in the Great War. I suspect you did as well, eh? What regiment?"

"The Rifles."

"Ralph and I were Highlanders. Mighty cold in a kilt in France."

"Honestly, it wasn't all that much better in trousers."

"True that. Now, Ralph says you might be interested in what I saw last Sunday night."

"Yes, sir." Lundin pulled out his notebook and started writing. "That would be 11 October."

"Hmmm. Guess so. I don't have a calendar handy. But it was just last Sunday, so I suppose it must be October 11. Anyhow, I was getting off shift. I make the evening meal and then leave the serving and the cleaning up to the night team. On Sundays we serve a late breakfast and then a late supper. No dinner. Most Sundays, the staff and the students only work a half day. It was kinda foggy that night. I walked to my jalopy and looked out over the lake. You can tell what the weather is going to be if you look back west along the lake. The fog was just rolling in. It was going to be a cold one that night."

Fleming chimed in, "We were out on the lake that night. It was a cold one for sure, and …"

Lundin looked at Fleming as if to say, "You are not helping." Fleming stopped in mid-sentence.

"Is that one a Brit? Is he one of the camp instructors?"

"No, Neal. He is just helping me with the investigation. He is from the Navy."

"Navy man, eh? Well, that means his compliment is more powerful stuff. The Navy feeds their sailors well. Hmmm." A puff of smoke came out of the pipe and out of the cook's mouth at the same time.

Lundin could have choked Fleming for distracting the cook. He looked up and patiently asked, "So, Sunday night."

"Ah, yeah. So, I'm walking to the jalopy, it's late. I see one of them radio guys headed to the lake. Odd that, eh? After all, it's dark, the fog is rolling in, and I rarely see them radio guys except at meals. He's one of the supervisors, see. Odd last name. I always called him Ned. He told me once he worked on the ore freighters. Hard life, that."

Lundin could see Fleming was getting impatient. This was always how witness statements progressed. You had to get the witness talking, and you absolutely had to let them wander about as they told their story. Interrupt them, and you usually had to start back from the beginning — if you hadn't lost them completely. Lundin nodded and said, "Life on the lakes is a hard one, that's sure."

"Yeah. So, I see him and wave. He waves back, but continues to the lake. You probably know there's no beach there. Just rocks and water. He looked like he was headed toward the rocks. It was just like that. Walking as if he was going to head right into the water."

At that point, Ralph said to the group, "How about we get a beer and sit down before the crowd comes for dinner."

"That's great, Ralph. The Mountie is paying, right?"

Lundin nodded. "OK, then a bump and a beer!"

Fleming asked, "A bump?"

Lundin whispered, "A shot of whiskey."

Fleming said to Ralph as he walked toward the bar, "One for me as well, Ralph!"

When the drinks were served and they were sitting around the table, Lundin politely worked back to the story. "Nate, you saw the radio guy go to the beach. Did he go in the water?"

The cook downed his shot of whiskey and took a sip of his beer. "Now Sergeant, that's just silly. Who is going to go into the water at night with all their clothes on, eh? Nope. He just walks along the shoreline until he meets up with a girl." Neal put his finger to the side of his nose and nodded. "That's why a man walks along the shoreline at night. To be with his sweetie, eh?"

If Lundin was surprised, he didn't show it. He asked, "You recognize the girl, Neal?"

"Oh sure. She's one of those folks training at the camp. Good lookin' girl. No wonder Novak was interested, eh?"

"You know her name?"

"Nah. The students come and the students go. I only recognize them by their numbers."

"Their numbers?"

"Yeah. You know, they wear their overalls sometimes into the mess hall. They got numbers painted on the back of the overalls. Don't ask me why. I guess it's to tell them apart. Truth is, no one is going to confuse that girl with any of the others. She was cute."

Lundin realized he was closing in on the story. He said, "Neal, what did you see once they met up?"

"They walked along the shoreline. I needed to get home. Last I saw, they were about a hundred yards east of the docks. I suspected they were going to find someplace…private." The cook's smile was crooked because of the pipe stem still planted on his lips.

"Neal, this is terrific. Thanks for helping." Lundin knew this was the last piece of the puzzle, and he needed to be sure his witness got this right. "Do you know the girl's number?"

"Oh sure, Sergeant. She's just about done with her training. She's number 010. I didn't see any of them today. I guess they are in their final training exercise. Probably return to camp tomorrow morning and get lunch. Dinner will be a big one. Lots of food and drink, and then they ship them off to the war. I hope they make it back. All good Canadians."

Neal finished his beer and stood up. "It's time for me to get home to Martha. Ralph, appreciate the beer. You take care of Charlotte, hear? And, Sergeant, you find the man who killed that radioman, OK? He was a polite guy. Always nice to me and the staff. He worked nights and never complained. I would see him at breakfast, tired as he could be. He didn't deserve to die in the lake. Not after his years on the freighters. Just wasn't right."

Lundin stood and shook the cook's hand. He said, "Mr. Dixon, thank you for your help. I reckon you have been the most helpful person I've talked to at the camp."

Dixon mumbled through his pipe. "Yeah, they are a closed-mouthed bunch out there. Never take the time to talk to any of us who work for them. I guess that's what you expect from the Brits." He paused and said, "Sorry, sir, but that's the truth."

Fleming nodded. "We can be a bit of a haughty bunch. I'm afraid I won't apologize for them. They were the same with me."

Dixon laughed. "Well, that just shows you it takes all kinds in this world. If they are willing to kill Nazis, I guess that's good enough for me." He shook Fleming's offered hand and walked away. His rubber boots squeaked along the wood floors. Ralph walked with him. Charlotte stayed for a moment.

"Ralph said you might be going out on the lake tonight with our boat. All we have is a trolling motor for a kicker. We could find another boat if you like."

"Ma'am, a boat with a trolling motor is just fine. We are simply going along the shoreline to look at where the victim fell into the water. Can we have an early dinner?"

"Ralph suspected you might ask. He thought you might want to get out on the lake right after you met with Neal. We have turkey soup and fresh bread ready. Will that work?"

"Soup, bread and coffee would be fantastic."

Fleming looked at Lundin and said, "And another…bump?"

"Ian, just one. Please."

Fleming called to Charlotte and said, "Could I have another whiskey…it's just for the damp, you understand."

Charlotte laughed. "Ralph always says the same. A short one for you then, along with your coffee."

The trolling motor quietly purred, taking the wooden rowboat toward the camp. The last remnants of daylight hung on behind them, with a dark blue horizon in the west. Lundin had already identified Venus rising. The weather forecast called for a clear, calm night. With luck, they would be back at the hotel before the moon set at midnight. The weather service said it was a waxing moon with more than 30 percent illumination. Plenty of light for navigation. However, also plenty to be identified by armed guards if they were caught at the camp.

After dinner, Fleming had put on his leather jacket. His rope-soled shoes offered a degree of silent passage far better than Lundin's boots. Lundin had pulled on a leather gilet vest with four pockets in the front and a large pocket in the back. As they loaded into the boat, Fleming asked, "Miles, have you ever picked a door lock? If not, I have my lockpick set issued at the camp."

Lundin smiled in the darkness. "Ian, I was probably picking locks when you were still in school. I had a…reckless youth."

"Hmmm, so I suppose I don't need to ask if you brought your revolver?"

"Another rather silly question, don't you think? When should a Mountie be without his firearm." He tapped the shoulder holster under his vest. "Now, what do you have to keep yourself safe?"

"I have an odd little item from our boffins. A tear-gas pen. Supposed to shoot a stream about five feet. Oh, and then there is a little item in my coat pocket. A gift from Colonel Donovan."

"A gift, eh?"

"A short-barrel .38 revolver. Not exactly government issue and certainly not something I would take into a warzone, but it will serve for tonight and then become a cherished memento. After all, it is a gift from America and will be my protector for tonight's adventure."

"Let's hope tonight doesn't end in a gunfight. The camp guards have Enfields and I suspect they will shoot first and ask questions later."

"Even better reason to be quick and quiet."

"Exactly. And, I think our quiet time is just around the corner." Lundin carefully pulled up on the shoreline and shut down the engine. Fleming got out with the bowline and pulled the boat under a set of overhanging branches of wild roses. Lundin pushed the stern of the boat up on the shore as well while Fleming knotted the line on a nearby tree.

Fleming whispered, "If you would like, I will be happy to lead us to the staff quarters. I have been creeping around the camp for over three weeks. I know a bit about the shadows."

Lundin replied, "That sounds good, Ian. Just remember, once we are close to the quarters we will abandon the shadows and walk naturally. No creeping at that point. This is the first rule of surveillance: if you act like you belong, everyone assumes you do belong."

"I will remember that. Still, my gran used to say: 'In the dark, all cats are grey.'"

"And, in case you wondered, if confronted I'm going to let you do the talking, since you belong here and I don't."

Fleming shook his head. "Brilliant."

The fog crept off the shoreline and began to swallow the camp. Lundin and Fleming sat against a half-dozen maple trees that were starting to drop their leaves. They watched and waited for a half hour to determine if there were patrols along the shoreline. There were none. In the distance there was an explosion, followed by some gunfire. Fleming whispered, "Given tonight is the final problem and that exercise takes place at the north end of the camp, I bet the entire training cadre as well as the camp guards are at that end of the camp to create a high degree of realism."

Lundin looked down at the radium hands of his watch. It was just after 8 p.m. He wanted their approach to seem natural, and he wanted to be certain that Stevens would still be working at HYDRA. He whispered to Fleming: "Time to go."

They broke out of the tree line and began a steady walk toward the barracks buildings. Before leaving the hotel, Lundin had checked his notes and his basic sketch map of the camp. He could identify the staff housing and the closest door. As they walked, Lundin said, "Ian, you need to slow down. I know the tension makes you want to break out into a run. It's natural, but you must fight it."

"You appear to have done this more than once."

"Stories for another time. But yes, I have done this sort of thing before."

They arrived at the staff quarters unnoticed. They entered the darkened hallway and walked directly to Novak's room. Once there, they turned around. There were two doors generally across the hallway from Novak. Fleming nervously whispered, "Which one?"

In Lundin's experience, there were always bumps in the road in an investigation, especially when it required what the Mounties politely called "night work." He hissed, "I take the left, you take the right. Try the door handle, gently. If it opens, take a look. Stevens isn't a careful dresser, so I suspect his room will be…"

"Got it. Unkempt room of a professor. I've been there."

Lundin nodded and walked to the left door. It was locked. He pulled out a small leather pouch from the front left pocket of the vest, unzipped it and took out a set of lock-picking tools. He dropped to one knee and started the process. It didn't take long. After all, the entire building looked to be temporary, and the door locks were even more so. As he was about to gain entry, he heard Fleming grunt.

Lundin saw Fleming on his back in a daze with blood trickling out of his nose. Lundin looked at a shadow running down the hall. As he started in pursuit, he heard the crack of a bullet whizz by his head. When he thought about it later, it seemed odd that he didn't hear the report of a gun, just the bullet passing by his ear. The time for clandestine night work was over. He drew his service Colt, took a knee and fired. The sound of the .45 filled the hallway. He saw the shadow stumble, grab his side and turn. Another three rounds whined over his head. Lundin accepted there would be little cover in this gunfight, but he took what was available and leaned against the open doorframe. He grabbed the shoulder of Fleming's flight jacket and pulled him close.

Fleming mumbled. "I'm fine, Miles. Get after the bastard."

Lundin nodded. "Since you are already here, can you check the room?"

Fleming wiped the blood from his nose with the back of his hand. He smirked. "Why not?"

Lundin took off down the hallway. He stopped at the doorframe leading out of the barracks. He had no idea if the shooter was waiting for him or not. He went down on one knee again and looked around the doorframe — revolver first, and then his head. In the gloom, there was no sign of the intruder. He raced down the field toward the lake. If the shooter was going to get away, he would have to follow the same route they did to enter the compound. He made it to the shoreline in time to see a motorboat with three men heading out into the lake. He took careful aim and fired two rounds at the motorboat engine. As his eyes recovered from the flash of his pistol, all he could see was the white wake of the boat as it pulled away. "Damnation," was all Lundin could say.

He put his revolver back in his shoulder holster and walked toward the barracks. As he walked back, he heard a gunshot in the distance. Clearly, the final problem continued well into the night. All the better for them as they made good their escape.

He found Fleming on his knees in the open doorway. He was bathed in the light from the single overhead lamp. "Are you OK?"

"I'm fine, but Stevens isn't."

"Hurt?"

"Dead. It looks like another broken neck. It isn't pretty, since his head is twisted completely around. I came into the room and tripped over him. I turned on the light to see if there was anything I could do."

Lundin decided in a split second. "Ian, we need to get out of here. We need to let the camp folks find Stevens and call us back to the scene. If we don't, the investigation will be completely compromised as they start to blame us for this mess." Lundin looked around the room. All of the drawers were pulled out of the dresser and the desk. Papers were strewn across the floor. It would take hours, if ever, to sort out what was missing. He said, "Come on, we have to get back to the hotel."

Fleming got up. He lost his footing and stumbled into Lundin. The Mountie grabbed his colleague by the shoulders and pulled him onto his shoulders. He said, "Now don't fidget, Ian. I'll carry you to the boat." Lundin started down the hallway and out the door with Fleming over his left shoulder. He was surprised how light Fleming was. While Fleming looked fit, his fitness regime must have been running or swimming. He had few muscles on his bones.

When they were finally in the boat and heading back to the hotel, Lundin said, "OK. As they say in the dime novels, we have made good our escape. If you can tell me what happened, that would be helpful."

Fleming sat on the deck in between the two rows of seats in the boat with his feet next to Lundin and his head leaning against the bow. He pulled a white handkerchief from his coat and pressed it against his nose. "Well, it's not like I haven't had my nose broken in the past."

Lundin nodded. "I suspect the intruder wasn't trying to break your nose. He was trying to kill you. I'm glad he wasn't successful."

Fleming's response was muffled. Lundin wasn't sure if he heard a laugh or a groan. Fleming pulled the handkerchief away from his face and said, "Well, we know for certain it wasn't Beatrice. The mug who hit me was taller and heavier than yours truly."

"Perhaps, but I'm certainly not going to scratch her off my list of suspects."

"Creed, then?"

"Ian, the entire affair has now changed course. The intruder was a professional, and he had some sort of silenced weapon. And, he had two colleagues in his boat. This wasn't supposed to be anything other than a simple elimination of what we can suspect was a loose end in a complex plot. We made it far more complicated for them."

"Professional?"

"During the days of prohibition in the US, there were plenty of villains who moved liquor across the lake to Buffalo. There were more than a few gunfights on our side of the border and in Buffalo. Different gangs fighting for control of that trade. Among those gangs were specialists in the violence."

"Murder incorporated?"

"Exactly. I saw a bit of this when I served in the Windsor barracks. The same sort of trade took place between Windsor and Detroit. But…" Lundin paused to think about how he wanted to frame the next sentence. He wasn't sure how Fleming might react. He decided to treat Fleming as he might any other trusted colleague. "I think this was something else entirely. I hate to admit it, but I'm beginning to believe you were right when you said this might lead us to a spy ring."

Fleming responded with another muffled comment. Laughter? Lundin thought it was possible. Lundin continued, "The good news is that I hit the villain. I'm not sure how badly he was hit, but a .45 can leave a pretty big hole no matter where it hits."

Fleming pulled the handkerchief away from his face. "He's going to need a doctor."

"Or his pals are going to need to dig a grave. I'm not sure which."

"I guess we got off easily."

"Let's see what happens when the camp folks find the body."

Another muffled comment ended the conversation as they pulled up toward the docks in Oshawa. Lundin said, "What?"

"I need a bourbon."

"I'll buy the first round."

The Investigation: Day Five
Too many victims

18 October 1942, Oshawa

CHAPTER EIGHTEEN —
TWO DEAD MEN, ONE BODY

Lundin had expected a call from the camp once Stevens' body was discovered. Instead, he woke up well before dawn after a restless night. He rarely had a peaceful night's sleep since the Great War. Too often, the sights, sounds, or smells of the trenches intruded in his dreams. This time the dream merged parts of the gunfight in the barracks with his time in the trenches. In his dream, the previous evening's shadow at the end of the hall was using a flamethrower to keep him from pursuing. When the shadow and the flamethrower disappeared, he found himself thigh deep in mud in a trench somewhere in France. He woke in a cold sweat.

From long experience, he knew he would not get back to sleep. So, he washed, shaved, polished his boots and changed into his uniform. The radium dial of his Elgin read: 4:45 a.m. He doubted anyone would be in the kitchen at that hour, but he left his room hoping to escape the horrors of his dream.

He was surprised once again to find Fleming in the restaurant. He had a mug of coffee in his hand and an empty glass which Lundin assumed had once held bourbon. "Ian, have you been up all night?"

"Miles, I dozed for a while, but my dreams were so grim I decided to come down and make myself useful. I made a pot of coffee and poured myself a drink. I've been sitting here for the last three hours trying to understand what happened last night." He took a sip of coffee and raised his left hand, which held four sheets of white paper. "Also, I have been trying to make sense of this."

Lundin walked over to the kitchen door where the coffee pot was on a warmer. He poured himself a mug and returned to the table. "I suppose you pilfered this from Stevens' room?"

"I prefer the term pinched, but the correct answer is yes. I took them from Stevens' body. They were folded up in his coat pocket next to his wallet."

"And what did you find?"

"I think it is a log of the various telegrams that HYDRA had received and sent over the past three days. Included in the mix are my messages to and from Room 39. And they are all deciphered. I hate to say it, but I think Stevens was a spy."

"For who?"

"I think the correct phrase is for whom."

"Don't be pedantic."

"Since I only have the paperwork of HYDRA, it is impossible to say who would have been the recipient. Given your conversation with Stevens, I suppose the most likely candidates would have been the Russians."

"If Stevens was a successful spy, who murdered him?"

"As I said when you first walked up, I have been trying to make sense of it all. There is a short note along with the papers." He pulled out a single sheet of letter paper and showed it to Lundin. It read:

B, this is my last delivery. Ned's death was too much. You know I want to help, but this is not the way. K

Lundin shook his head. "So, we can assume B is Beatrice?"

"I think so, but how does this all fit? After all, Thomas has been in training with me for weeks. How would she use this sort of information?"

Lundin tried to work out an answer. "Remember the map with the x marks on the beach? Perhaps she met someone on the beach. What is curious is that we haven't heard from the camp yet. Do you think they intend to make Stevens' body just disappear?"

"And, precisely who do you think might make Stevens disappear? And how? Another body in the lake?"

"If so, they better weigh it down this time." Lundin stared at his coffee mug as if it might contain more answers. "You do realize I am going to have to report the entire story to my chief."

"Miles, you might follow a rule that I have used in Room 39 when delivering difficult news to my boss. The rule is: everything you tell your boss must be completely true. However, it doesn't always have to be truly complete."

Lundin smiled and said, "We have a similar way of looking at things. I thought it might not be useful to explain our plan to break into Stevens' quarters. And, since we don't have the full picture yet, it might be appropriate to stay relatively vague about the entire misadventure. After all, the chief is going to ask what the camp leaders think about the entire event. Since we don't know that answer, it might be best to delay the conversation completely."

"A wise decision."

"I've been accused over time of playing on the edge of regulations for a successful arrest. This might be another one of those cases."

"So, what happens next?"

"I think we go back to the camp this morning. I would expect something will happen when we arrive."

"Something that doesn't involve spending time in jail?"

"Indeed. Of course, you are traveling with the RCMP. We are the ones who put people in jail. It seems unlikely they will link us to anything that happened last night."

"We can only hope."

"Ian, what we can do before breakfast is consider what the camp cook told us last night. Why would Novak be walking on the shore with Thomas? They shouldn't have known each other, and certainly wouldn't have been…courting."

Fleming laughed. "Courting? Really, Miles? Still, I agree with you that the eyewitness statement makes Thomas the last person to see Novak alive."

"Usually, the last person is the murderer."

"I can tell you one thing. Thomas certainly could have broken his neck. She has all the necessary training. But why would she?"

"I think she is the only one who can answer that question. Still, let's remember that Novak had the map in his shoe. Could he have interrupted something?"

They sat pondering the puzzle until the cook and waitress arrived. As soon as she had her apron on, Charlotte walked up to the table. She said, "You made the coffee this morning?"

Lundin said sheepishly, "We got up early and we know how to make coffee. I hope that's OK?"

"Don't matter to me what folks do before I arrive. After I'm here, then it's another story. You guys are the only ones this morning, so let me know what you would like for breakfast. About two hours after you left in the boat, the other three guests checked out. Left in a hurry. They didn't even want dinner. Ralph thinks they were New Yorkers. Always in a hurry, those folks."

"Three guys?"

"Yup. Just stayed one full night. Of course, they paid for two because you must pay if you stay in your room after noon. I will clean up their room today, though October isn't exactly a busy month for us. Strange, eh? Why would you drive to New York at night?"

Fleming nodded. "Strange indeed."

Charlotte was headed back to the kitchen when the telephone rang. She said, "Oh, bother. Who is going to call at this time in the morning?"

Fleming looked at Lundin. "Who could it be?"

The waitress called from the kitchen. "Sergeant, it's your office in Toronto."

As Lundin stood up, he whispered to Fleming, "This can't be good." He walked over to the kitchen. The phone in the kitchen was the old style, with a speaking horn attached to the wooden box on the wall and a separate earpiece, attached with a wire. He stood close to the horn, held the earpiece to his ear and said, "Lundin."

The voice of his sergeant major boomed through the earpiece. "Lundin, up already. Good. You have another body down there."

Lundin tried to sound surprised. "Really?"

"Don't play with me, Lundin. I just got off the phone with the local constable. He just delivered the body to the coroner. The body washed up on the lake shore. This time there's a large bullet hole in his chest. You know anything about that, Lundin?"

"Sergeant Major, I'll head to the coroner immediately and see what's going on."

"You didn't answer my question, Senior Sergeant."

"I don't have enough information yet to answer accurately, Sergeant Major. After all, it is hunting season and a hunting rifle could make a big hole."

"So could a Mountie's .45."

"I'll get on it right now. I will call you back once I've sorted it all out."

"Any success with your other murder?"

"We are closing in on a couple of suspects. It isn't going to be pretty. They are both part of the camp."

Lundin heard the sergeant major's laugh. "That's why the chief sent you, Lundin. You are so good at handling sensitive cases. Sort it and sort it soon!" The line went dead before Lundin could say anything else.

He looked over at the waitress and her husband. They had been watching him for the entire conversation. He said, "We need to get started soon. Any chance of a quick breakfast?"

Ralph turned back to his grill station. He said over his shoulder, "Eggs and bacon shortly. Sound good?"

"Eggs, bacon and toast for two sounds great. Thanks."

Fleming had filled their coffee cups while he was waiting. He said, "So, they finally reported Stevens' body?"

"I don't think so. I think the local constable found a different body."

"Big hole, about the size of a .45?"

"Might be. It looks like we need to visit our coroner soonest. Breakfast first, because I have no idea when we will eat again after we leave here today."

Fleming puffed on one of his cigarettes. "You know, Miles, it's always an adventure with you."

It was dark the entire drive to Sutton's home. The large headlamps on the Buick cut a yellow beam through the fog as they drove along the lake. Lundin was in a hurry, but he was a cautious driver during the early morning. He had witnessed too many accidents caused by deer crossing roads just before dawn. That was especially true during hunting season. The last thing he needed was an accident report and a mangled car along with what was now an investigation with three bodies. Fleming looked over at Lundin's face illuminated by the yellow glow of the instrument panel. He said, "Miles, I know you don't like to talk while driving, but I would like to know something."

Lundin grunted. Fleming took that to be an agreement to continue. "What I would like to know is what we intend to say to Sutton when we see him. I mean, if the body is our shooter from last night, Sutton is going to have dug a .45 slug out of him. He's going to know it isn't a hunting accident."

Lundin growled and then said, "Ian, let's not jump to conclusions. All my sergeant major said was a big hole. If it is my round, we will have to sort out an answer then. But you trained on .45s at the camp, right? Pistols, some Canadian military revolvers and even Tommy guns are chambered in .45. So, there is no reason for Sutton to assume it came from my revolver. And, even if it is our shooter, what's to say that his compatriots didn't put a round in him and push him over the side of the boat? We just don't know what evidence there will be until we see it."

"Fair point, Miles. I guess I was just thinking about contingencies."

"Contingencies are fine in combat, but this is just another crime. I've said it before: we just follow the evidence. No telling where it might lead." Lundin smiled and said, "And you need to think positively. After all, the good doctor will be offering you a cup of tea."

"You really know how to hurt a man."

They pulled the Buick into Sutton's driveway just as a local ambulance pulled away. The sun was starting to appear, cutting through grey clouds to the south and west. Lundin turned to Fleming. "It's going to be a bad weather day today. I hope you have a slicker as well as your flight jacket."

"The camp issued a waxed cotton coat that somehow I forgot to return. I'm pretty certain they aren't going to ask for it back."

"All good. When we go back to Oshawa and before we return to the camp, we'll stop and pick it up. Mine is already in the trunk."

"You mean the boot?"

Lundin shook his head. "Whatever." He walked up to Sutton's door and rapped three times. From inside he heard Sutton acknowledge the knock. The doctor was in shirt sleeves and wool trousers. He was unshaven and he looked tired. Lundin said, "Apologies, doctor. My bosses wanted me to meet you as soon as possible. I understand we have another body."

Sutton nodded and said, "Come in, gents. You look like I feel. A long night, eh?"

Fleming nodded. "A long few days, sir."

"Well come in. I'll put the kettle on. We'll have some tea and if you like, some toast."

Before Fleming could say anything, Lundin said, "Sir, that would be grand." He and Fleming walked through the living room and into the study. Lundin took his place in front of the desk while Fleming did a turn around the room.

"You know, Sutton is a Navy man through and through. He has photos of two different ships from the Great War. A destroyer and a cruiser. The Navy didn't have much surface warfare after Jutland, but they had plenty of difficulties with German U-boats. Repeated in this war."

Lundin nodded. "In 1914, my father wanted me to join the Navy instead of the Army. I couldn't see myself on a ship in the Atlantic waiting to be torpedoed."

Fleming laughed. "Good choice, because a man your size wouldn't have fit in any ship I have ever seen."

From the doorway, Sutton's voice added, "I agree completely. I often thought that the Navy should have a height limit for all sailors. Otherwise, a man like Sergeant Lundin would be knocking his head on bulkheads and stairwells every day. I treated more than a few injuries on my ships, and most were from tall men in small compartments." He set down a tray with mugs, a tea pot and a plate of buttered toast. "Help yourselves, gentlemen. We have a bit to talk about."

Sutton poured his tea, sighing as he settled into the oak chair behind his desk. "I have been the coroner's special advisor for three years. There have been plenty of accidental deaths, but only one case of manslaughter. Now, I receive two murder victims in two days."

Lundin put down his mug and asked a question, though he suspected he knew the answer. "Another from Camp X?"

Another sigh from the doctor, and then an answer that surprised them both. "Another death and another Canadian sailor."

Fleming's head shot up like he had been hit with an electric shock. "A sailor?"

"Commander, I'm sure you know that the camp serves as a commando training camp for all services. The victim this time was a sailor. He had a tattoo on his forearm associated with the lake freighter union and still had his identity tags around his neck. Canadian Navy tags."

Lundin was afraid of the answer when he asked. "Sir, his name?"

"Jovanovic. He was a machinist mate in the Canadian Navy." Sutton looked over at Fleming. "Commander, you have gone white. Take some tea, man."

Fleming said, "Sir, I trained with Jovanovic just last week. He was a good sailor and a loyal Canadian."

"I have no doubt, Commander. Training for war has its own dangers, but I don't expect you think this was a training accident."

Lundin shook his head. "Sir, I will defer to you on this. I'm a simple Mountie who makes few assumptions."

Sutton laughed. "Sergeant, I doubt you are a simple Mountie. But I appreciate your caution in jumping to conclusions. Here is what I know: Jovanovic had no water in his lungs. He was dead when he was thrown into the lake. Like Novak, he first sustained a violent punch to incapacitate him. This time, it was a punch to the solar plexus that broke his sternum. He would have been struggling to breathe when he was killed."

"How did he die?"

"Even the constable made the correct assessment. He had a bullet hole about the size of my thumb that went through his chest and exited just above his shoulder. It was not pretty."

"Any other evidence on the body?"

"The lake takes its share. I'm afraid I can't help you the way I did with Novak. He was wearing a heavy sweater and a set of khaki overalls and work boots. I can say that the shot was point-blank, possibly pushed directly against his chest. His sweater and overalls were burned from the gunshot. What is curious at this point is that I haven't heard anything from the camp. Jovanovic drifted ashore near Oshawa, and the local constabulary brought him here before taking him to the morgue. They assumed he was from the camp, but since he was found in their jurisdiction they brought him to me first. They called your headquarters and were told to let you report the news to the camp. You would think the trainers would have noticed one of their students was missing, eh?"

Fleming still looked pale. He said, "You examined him here?"

"Well, not precisely here, Commander. I have a small surgery in the back of the house. But I wasn't about to refuse. They were at my door before I knew what was happening."

"Doctor, I know you haven't done a complete exam, but can you tell me if you think Jovanovic was sitting or standing when he was shot?"

"Sergeant, that's impossible to say at present. The trajectory from the entry wound to the exit wound argues that the gun was aiming upwards when he was shot. He could have been standing and his assailant sitting when he shot the victim or his assailant could have been a smaller man. I don't think any further examination will answer that question."

Lundin carefully placed his mug on the tea tray and stood up. "Sir,

I think we will leave you in peace. For now, I need to get back to the Camp X and try to determine what happened to our Canadian."

Sutton nodded. "He deserves justice, Sergeant."

Fleming stood up and placed his mug on the tray. "Sir, if I have anything to say about it, I promise he will have justice."

"Commander, I know what sort of justice the Navy would prefer, but this was not a crime committed on one of His Majesty's ships. Please remember that."

Fleming acknowledged Sutton's comment with a simple, "Aye, sir." He turned and walked out.

Sutton said to Lundin, "Watch that man, Sergeant. He is looking for revenge rather than justice. I don't want to see the commander in the morgue or standing in the dock as an accused killer."

Lundin said, "Agreed, sir. I think this may be the first time Commander Fleming has seen a colleague killed. I suspect it will not be his last. I just need to stay by his side for a bit while he realizes this is a fact of life in war. Thank you for your insight and for the tea. We had best get to work."

Sutton offered his hand and Lundin took it. "Good luck, Sergeant. You probably don't need any luck, but it's all this old Navy man can offer."

"I always need a little luck, sir. In this case, I need plenty of luck to sort through two murders. I will let myself out, sir." With that, Lundin walked out of the study, through the living room and out the door toward the Buick.

As they left Sutton's driveway, Lundin could see Fleming was furious. For once he was quiet, and his face seemed cast in stone. He stared out the windshield with exaggerated concentration. Lundin was fully comfortable with the silence, but he wondered when Fleming might explode in anger. Finally, the eruption began.

"What did Jovanovic ever do to any of these people? He was a man who simply wanted to serve his country and fight the Nazis." Lundin knew from experience that there wasn't much he could say that would help, so he waited for Fleming's next comment. "A .45 to the chest! What a horror! Clearly this is the work of that bastard Creed. He must hate Yugos, or was afraid Novak told Jovanovic something about his time in the Balkans."

Lundin let Fleming stew in his thoughts for a minute and then decided to intercede. "Ian, we don't know that. In fact, we can't say that Creed had anything to do with any of the three murders. Let's not forget that Stevens had nothing to do with Creed at all."

"But he is the most likely suspect. He has the skills; he has access to weapons, and he has a motive."

"Ian, let's review the evidence. The only connection we can see between Novak and Jovanovic is their ethnicity. There is a direct link between Novak and Stevens which points to some sort of link to HYDRA. There is the mysterious concealment in a coin. Now, other than an eyewitness report of Novak meeting with Thomas, we don't have any tie between HYDRA and the training program. And, don't forget our little gunfight in Stevens' quarters and the letter you recovered last night, which we presume was between Stevens and Thomas. It is definitely a puzzle."

"I can add one thing to your list. I rarely saw Jovanovic talk to Thomas. He was a shy man and definitely not about to chat with officers of any gender. But after Novak's death, I saw him talk to Thomas twice during our training in the house of horrors."

Lundin nodded. "I saw that as well. I just thought it was some flirting between the two."

"Miles, I know what flirting looks like. I happen to be quite a master at it. The conversations I saw between those two were far from flirting."

"Another piece of the puzzle, no?"

Fleming returned to his grim demeanor. "I just want to know what sort of beast is doing this killing? Always up close. It seems so … personal."

"Ian, if you will accept my experience as a measure of mankind, I can tell you that murder is always up close and personal. Combat is different. You have a man in your gunsight, but usually he is yards, sometimes hundreds of yards away. He hardly looks human. You pull the trigger and you watch him fall. Later, you might march past his body, but by then he is a grey, inanimate object, hardly human at all."

Lundin paused as he stared through the Buick windshield into the morning sun. "Murder is different. The murderer has the victim in front of him. He watches life leave the victim as he does violence against the man. If the murder is in the heat of the moment, after the fact the killer is horrified at what he has done. If the murder is planned, the perpetrator relishes his success. Three murders in one place means the murderer or murderers are comfortable with death. Perhaps Novak's death was an accident, though I suspect not. The last two were clearly planned, and our murderer has a taste for death. This person has killed in the past, well before Novak. Like a dog with rabies, he will kill again and again if we don't stop him."

"But why?"

"Every case is different, Ian. The motivation is internal; the murderer knows why. We can only guess until he is caught and interrogated." Lundin pulled the Buick off the road. He turned to Fleming and said, "I think I have an idea."

"Who?"

"Not so much who as why."

"Miles, this is not a good time to play with me. I am quite angry over the loss of Petyr."

Lundin nodded. "OK. I have been focused on the camp and on Novak's background. The story of Novak and Novosel, and now another Yugoslav Jovanovic, seemed such a straight-line connection. Stevens helped direct us toward this link as well."

"And now Stevens is dead."

"Ian, that's exactly the point. What if the centerpiece of this was HYDRA?"

"When we first talked, I told you it might be a spy tale."

"I know, and I was too focused on the usual reasons for murder. What if there is an espionage connection?"

"Nazis in Canada?"

"Not Nazis, Ian. Bolsheviks."

Fleming looked out his window across the fields and to the distant lake. "I can see how the Soviets would want to know what messages were passing between London and New York. Especially if there is an eventual link between London and Washington. The Soviets are worried that we will cut some sort of deal with the Germans and turn on Stalin and his cronies."

"I'm no ally of the Bolshies, but we did fight them right after the Great War. The UK, Canada and the US all supported the Whites. And let's not forget that Stalin spent the early part of the war avoiding a conflict with Hitler. I think it's all about HYDRA."

For once, it was Fleming who was unconvinced. "That's a fine theory. Now where is the evidence you are always telling me must drive the investigation?"

"Stevens admitted to me that he was a supporter of the Soviet Union. We know there was something going on with the concealment inside the coin. You said the operators in HYDRA saw Stevens hunting for his lucky coin. And you found papers in Stevens' room that looked like communication logs for HYDRA. There is no good reason for any of this except some sort of espionage."

"You think Novak was the traitor?"

Lundin shook his head. "I think Novak uncovered something and he had to be silenced."

"What about Stevens?"

"I wonder if his conscience got to him. Stevens might have been a socialist, and he might even have been willing to give secrets to the Soviets. He probably thought he was just supporting an ally in the fight against the Nazis. I suspect he realized what a dangerous game this was when he found out Novak was killed. He was appalled. He was an academic, after all. Before Novak was killed, it was all about supporting the workers' paradise. And, suddenly, it wasn't about the workers at all. If he was about to tell us the entire story, that might be enough for him to be…as you said before, eliminated."

"That must mean they have another spy in HYDRA."

"Or, they may have used the information that they gathered from

HYDRA to gain access in another way. Or, they simply want to erase the problem and start someplace new."

"In Room 39, we have talked for some time about tapping international cables that route through the US. It is one of the taskings we sent to Stephenson. If HYDRA merely passed the wireless traffic to the Canadian-US telegraph cables, the Soviets might have found that a technical solution was more valuable than a spy."

"So, Stevens might have become expendable."

"Miles, you've convinced me. But it still doesn't tell me who the murderer is."

"Ian, I think you might know her already."

"Her?"

"Who is the other person linked to all three men? Only Thomas."

"She has killed all three?"

"You were the one who told me that Camp X teaches these techniques."

"True, but a woman?"

"I've arrested more than a few women who killed lovers, husbands, attackers, even their children. Murderers don't have to be men."

"I won't believe it unless she admits to it."

"Ian, first we have to catch her."

"You don't expect she will return to the camp, do you?"

"I don't, and we have a real challenge because we have a suspect, or possibly a member of a conspiracy, who is also a pilot."

"Why are we sitting here?"

Lundin reached up on the column to the shift lever, put the Buick in gear and said, "Why, indeed?"

CHAPTER NINETEEN — CHAOS AT THE CAMP

As he pulled the Buick toward the camp entrance, Lundin said, "Ian, if they give us a hard time, I'm just going to run the guards over and break through the gate. I'm tired of being kept at arm's length in this case."

Fleming nodded. "Agreed." But this time, the guards lifted the barrier as soon as they saw the Buick approach. "It would appear that someone has decided there is value in having you on post," Fleming added.

Lundin didn't comment and just accelerated through the gate, driving to camp headquarters. Before he got out, he saw Creed come running out the door and down the stairs. Creed shouted, "Miles, you are just in time. We have another dead body."

Lundin got out of the Buick and put on his Stetson. "I know."

"How could you know? We just found him."

Fleming couldn't miss the opening. "Captain, we were just at the coroner's office looking at him."

Creed looked stunned. "Who? Certainly not Stevens. His body is still on post at the clinic."

Lundin gave Fleming a quick glance and then said, "Hamish, we were just at the coroner's home. He completed a brief exam of one of your students found floating in the lake. I met him when I first arrived, a Navy machinist mate named Jovanovic. He was shot and dumped into the lake."

Lundin carefully watched Creed's reaction. The color drained out of his face, and he took a step back. Either the man was an exceptional actor or he was totally stunned. "Jovanovic? He is still out on the final exercise. The students should be returning this morning. The exercise ends with a road march to camp." He looked at his watch. "They should be here in less than an hour."

Before Creed could recover, Lundin asked, "What about Stevens? He's dead? What happened?"

"It looks like he slipped or tripped in his room. Broke his neck. That will put HYDRA in a mess. Given their importance and secrecy, we need your help as an RCMP Mountie to formalize the clinic's findings."

Fleming said in his best Royal Navy manner, "Captain, don't you think the death of two men from the same office just a bit suspicious?"

Creed looked at Fleming in a way that promised violence. Lundin intervened. "I think what the commander is saying is that I will need to take a very hard look at the circumstances of Mr. Stevens' death and consider the evidence in the context of Mr. Novak's death."

Creed seemed to recover. "Apples and oranges, Miles."

Fleming decided to get in the last word. "Both fruit, Captain."

Before the two men started to wrestle each other to the ground, Lundin said, "Hamish, here's what we need to do. I need you to give an order to whoever you have who controls the approach to the camp. I want you to hold the students someplace under Commander Fleming's authority until we can start to question them about Jovanovic. In the meantime, you need to take me to the clinic so that I can see Stevens' body, and then we will go to Stevens' room to determine the circumstances of his death." Lundin paused. "Of course, if you would prefer to take this up the chain of command through to the governor general or to Mr. Stephenson, that is fine by me. After all, it is still early. I can simply wait with Commander Fleming for the arrival of the students."

Lundin could see Creed make the mental calculations regarding what chance he or the Camp X commander might have in preventing an RCMP investigation. While he was making those calculations, Lundin stood in front of him, staring down at him from under his

Stetson. After nearly a minute, Creed made up his mind. "Wait here while I gather one of the junior instructors and give him the proper orders. Then we will walk over to the clinic."

As Creed walked away, Fleming said, "I suspect he was afraid you would bop him one before he could say anything. You do know you are a rather imposing fellow, eh?"

"It's the Stetson, Ian. The Stetson always does the trick."

"I will remember that."

"Now, when you and his junior officer start to gather the students, do your best not to let them know why they are being prevented from getting back to barracks."

"That will be easy, Miles. The instructors here are always making life hard for the students. They seem to think that brutalizing the students is character-building."

"Well, whatever it might seem, we don't want them to know what is going on. I need you to charm Creed's junior and the students as well."

"I can do that."

"I never had any doubt. Also, your commander's uniform and your black eye from last night's fight should encourage them to obey instructions."

"If only I had a Stetson."

Creed came down the steps from the headquarters with a young lieutenant in tow. Lundin whispered to Fleming, "Ian, don't push it."

Lundin and Creed walked in silence. As they approached one of the buildings with a door marked with a red cross, Creed finally said, "You don't think Stevens' death was an accident?"

"Do you? After all, you were the one who said Novak's death was an accident, and we both know that wasn't the case."

"It was what the camp commander wanted as the official position. I just obeyed orders."

Lundin paused in front of the door and asked, "Were you following orders when you attacked me and stole Novak's papers?"

Creed looked stunned. Lundin knew it was a bluff and wondered how Creed would answer. He received the answer he expected, the initial denial most criminals offered when confronted. "I can't imagine what you are talking about."

"Hamish, from the beginning you and the camp command have worked hard to limit my access to facts that might be embarrassing or might undermine your mission. I'm not at all surprised. After all, the RCMP is often involved in sensitive matters where officials would prefer not to have the complete story revealed in court or in the papers. I suspect you both wanted to be sure that the correspondence between Commando Novosel and his friend Ned Novak was not revealed during my investigation. The camp commander was only concerned that Novak's death and Novosel's correspondence would undermine the mission of the camp."

Lundin paused and posed a question. "Or, were you only interested in how the letters might embarrass you?"

Creed looked like he had been punched in the gut. He croaked, "And why do you think it was me?"

"Please, don't waste my time. It was you because only you knew that I was going to search Novak's quarters and, honestly, if my attacker had been the one who killed Novak, Stevens and Jovanovic, I would be another dead body. You knocked me out using a technique that needed precision and experience. A few more seconds of whatever you used on me and I would have been dead."

"It was important that the Yugoslavia mission wasn't compromised."

"And if you trusted me from the beginning, it is entirely possible that Jovanovic would be alive and on his way to the Yugoslavia mission."

"What are you going to do now?"

"I'm going to find the killer. The rest is not my concern, or the concern of the RCMP or the Canadian government. Assaulting a member of the RCMP is an offense, but not one that I am going to put forward. Canada fully supports your mission here, and we have no interest in disrupting the training. You and your commander will have to decide what you want to do about the Novosel correspondence." Lundin paused and turned away from the clinic door. "Now, tell me the truth about Stevens' death. Not an accident, correct?"

"Not an accident, Miles."

"Broken neck, just like Novak?"

"Yes."

Lundin was no longer using his collegial tone. He was in full interrogator mode when he asked, "Do we need to visit Stevens' quarters now, or have you already checked? Searched by the murderer, correct?"

"The HYDRA military police reported that his room was turned upside down. The murderer was searching for something. We don't know what."

"That's all I needed to know for now. Let's head back to Fleming and your lieutenant. We have a murderer to catch."

"One of our students?"

"All I can say at present is one of your students is either a suspect or a witness."

"Who?"

"Flight Lieutenant Beatrice Thomas."

For the third time that morning, Creed lost color in his face.

Lundin shook his head. "I suppose she charmed you."

"We are not supposed to fraternize with the students."

"But you did."

"When we could."

"Hamish, for God's sake, you didn't talk about other students or their future missions, did you?"

Creed blushed. "She asked about my missions, and I told her about Yugoslavia. I told her about the challenges of working with the Chetniks and the Partisans and how they were always at each other's throats. I told her about how I thought Jovanovic might help us gain some traction with the Chetniks and possibly help us moderate those problems." He looked up at Lundin. "Did you know that he was a distant relative of the leader of the Chetniks, General Mihailovich? He could have been a way forward with the Yugoslav Royalists."

"Was Thomas headed to Yugoslavia?"

"I doubt it. Her language skills are French and Spanish. If she passes through the finishing school in Britain, she will be headed to France, most likely southern France."

"Almighty God, Hamish! Alright, let's find her and get her into custody."

"But she can't have killed those men."

"Why?"

Creed blushed again. "She was with me the night Novak died."

"All night?"

"No, she came to my quarters late."

"After she killed Novak and pushed him into the lake."

"And Stevens? She was already on the final exercise."

"Stevens is another story. I suspect she had conspirators."

"Other students?"

"More likely outsiders. We won't know until we have a conversation with the flight lieutenant."

Creed was silent as they walked across the parade grounds toward the area where Fleming was waiting. The students were straggling in after the long road march, wearing rucksacks and carrying rifles. They look exhausted. Creed offered, "I know the last exercise. I will ask some of the students when they last saw Number 010. In the meantime, I'm sure the camp commander as well as the HYDRA chief would want you to check Stevens' room. He is…was right across the hall from Novak. I will see you there."

Lundin nodded and watched Creed as he walked away. Creed seemed to go quickly from denial to a sullen acceptance that he was part of something he did not understand.

This was the first time Lundin had investigated espionage, but not the first time he had uncovered some government or military senior duped by criminals or lured into a sexual trap. After the initial confrontation, most would cooperate to avoid prosecution. Sometimes they were angry but, most of the time, they worked hard to forget their part in the crime. Creed had broken no laws, but he had certainly bent regulations and probably damaged a future SOE operation. As Lundin had said to Creed, that was not an RCMP problem. As far as he was concerned, it was a problem for Creed's conscience and nothing more.

Lundin approached Fleming as Creed walked over to his lieutenant. Fleming asked, "Does he know?"

"He knows now. He was foolish."

"The communists call them useful idiots."

"That too. I will explain when we finally get our hands on Thomas. Creed says he is going to help. In the meantime, he wants us to check Stevens' room. He gave me directions, so it looks like they don't know we were here last night."

"At least that's something."

***

Stevens' room looked nothing like the chaos they had seen last night. Lundin thought it looked way too clean and tidy for Stevens. Most probably the work of the HYDRA military policemen, one of whom was standing at the door. Lundin said, "Sergeant, we are here at the request of the camp commander and the HYDRA chief. We are going to check Mr. Stevens' room."

"Yes, Sergeant. We've already done a check. Not much to see. Mr. Stevens kept a squared away room."

"It appears so. Still, you never know what you can find if you look hard enough."

Before the sergeant could comment, Fleming walked up. The military policeman recognized the Navy commander and came to the position of attention. Fleming said, "Stand at ease, Sergeant. We are just making the necessary protocol checks. I'm sure you understand."

The sergeant relaxed and said, "Sir, I've been an MP for a while. There are always protocol checks, especially when you are talking about VIPs."

"Indeed. Now, you don't need to look over our shoulders, but it would be good if you blocked the door so any of the other residents don't get in our way. You know how civilians are…always gawking at life's tragedies."

The MP came to attention. "Sir!" He allowed Fleming to pass and then stood with his back to the room facing the hallway. He looked like he intended to exert authority if anyone tried to intrude.

Fleming saw Lundin smiling. He held his finger to the side of his nose. Normally a reasonable gesture of shared confidence. This time, it made him wince. He had forgotten completely about his broken nose.

Lundin was on his hands and knees running his fingers along the floorboards. Fleming knew if he asked, he would draw the MP's attention. Instead, he simply walked around the room in the opposite direction and said loud enough for the MP to hear, "Sergeant, it looks like there is nothing to see here."

Lundin played his role. "I know," he said. "Just give me a minute and then we will be gone." He had found what he was looking for — a loose floorboard next to the armoire. He used his penknife to pry up the board and reached into the cavity below. There was a small packet wrapped in brown paper. He placed it in his pocket, replaced the floorboard and stood up, then spoke to both Fleming and the MP. "All good. As the sergeant said, Stevens kept a clean room. Poor fellow."

As he walked past the sergeant, he said, "Thanks for letting us do the needful. I'm sure they told you to keep an eye out for anyone who intends to pilfer the room. There isn't much there, but you never know if someone might be tempted to steal from a dead man."

"Exactly so, Sergeant. That's exactly what my sergeant said as well."

Lundin nodded and walked out. He turned toward the door that faced the camp rather than the one at the other end of the hallway that faced the lake. As he walked, he carefully looked at the doorframe and wall. Fleming was right behind him and said, "Looking for something?"

"Bullets from last night. At least two from a silenced pistol."

"If the door was open, they could be anywhere."

"But I reckon it was closed. Do me a favor when we get to the door and let me open it for you. It will give us a chance to look at the door in sunlight."

Fleming did as he was asked. From the MP's perspective, it looked like the Mountie was giving the Royal Navy officer the sort of polite courtesy he would have given the officer. Instead, it allowed Lundin to step out into the sunlight with the door wide open while Fleming walked out. Lundin had his pen knife out again and quickly pried a bullet from the door. It had almost gone all the way through, so he pried it from the outside rather than the inside of the door. The lead round captured in his hand, he closed the door and walked toward Fleming. "As I suspected, a small round. Hard to silence a heavy pistol."

"Donovan showed Godfrey a pistol his boffins have designed. Nearly silent except for the sound of the bolt. A .22 caliber. Only good at short range."

"Like from one end of the hall to another. So you reckon it was a US pistol?"

"I know little about Russian pistols or their work at silencers."

Lundin said, "I know the American gangs didn't care a hoot about silencing their pistols or Tommy guns. If they wanted a quiet killing, they did close work with screwdrivers and ice picks."

"Creative bunch, those American thugs."

"I guess this just adds to our complicated set of events. I hope we get something useful from Creed."

"Do you think he will give up Thomas?"

"It could go either way. If he feels like he was duped, he will. If he was part of the con, then we are going to be looking for him as well."

CHAPTER TWENTY —
TO CATCH A SPY

As they walked back to the Buick, Creed drove up in one of the camp jeeps. He looked better than he had when they last saw him. Now he looked more angry than dismayed. Lundin had seen this transformation in the past. At first, the individual targeted was hurt and embarrassed that he could be fooled and taken advantage of by a con man. Eventually, the target — or, in villains' parlance, the sucker — transferred that emotion to anger against the villain. Lundin realized that he would need to keep a close eye on Creed. Thomas was a dangerous person, but Creed was also an expert in the art of close combat; given an opportunity, he might be tempted to go from disabling her to killing her. Lundin turned to Fleming and whispered, "If we capture Thomas, keep an eye on Creed to be sure he doesn't do her harm. We want her alive and in RCMP custody."

Fleming nodded. "My guess is Creed has a plan to punish his former lover."

"Just so. And I suspect you have a plan to do harm to Thomas as well, so I'm watching you, Ian."

Lundin turned to Creed. "Have you sorted out where Thomas is?"

Creed shouted from the jeep, "She never returned with her team. She and Jovanovic are missing. The last anyone saw either of them was when they started their road march back to camp. The team wasn't all that interested. They all went back to the barracks to clean up and intended to celebrate. Apparently, Thomas was central to the success of their training mission."

Fleming whispered, "Of course she was."

Lundin thought for a minute. It seemed likely that Thomas was trying to escape. If that was so, what were the most likely venues? Certainly not cross country on foot. Take a camp vehicle? Hardly likely, since the jeeps were rugged but not fast. His mind raced as he thought of other options. He said to Creed, "Do you have any speedboats at the camp?"

Creed shook his head. "We have a couple of safety boats we use when we train the students in folboat operations, but they are flat-bottomed rowboats with small engines. I'm not sure they could even survive in the lake."

"Are the folboats secured?"

Creed was about to say something like "Why would we?" He stopped himself and said, "No." He put the jeep in gear and tore across the parade ground toward the lake. Lundin and Fleming jumped into the Buick and followed.

As they raced along the dirt road following Creed, Fleming shouted, "It would be a very hard row to get anywhere in a folboat. Jovanovic and I worked hard along the shoreline and only covered a few miles in a night-long row."

Lundin shouted back, "If her confederates are waiting someplace close, she could meet them outside the camp wire. They can be in a car and headed almost anywhere in Canada in less than an hour on the coast road. And, if they have a powerboat, they can be in the US before we sort out what happened. We need to catch her before then. Otherwise, we will either lose her or it will be a gunfight with more than Thomas shooting at us."

Before they could continue the conversation, Creed's jeep had pulled off the dirt road to a track that led directly to the lake. The grey sky made the lake look even more ominous. An October storm was edging eastward, and the lake was filled with choppy water. Before the jeep had stopped, Creed jumped out and headed toward the small boathouse where the folboats were kept. A short driveway headed toward a pier where Lundin could see a moored boat with a small engine. "At least that's something," he said, more to himself than to Fleming.

Lundin parked the Buick next to the jeep, jumped out and ran toward the boathouse. He met Creed coming out. "All the folboats are there and dry. No sign of entry since the last time we used the boats five days ago."

Lundin looked around as Fleming approached from the lake. "I looked down at the dock. Someone used the dock recently. There are water splashes next to the camp boat and on the dock. We're too late."

Creed shouted over the growing wind from the storm, "What do we do now?"

Lundin paused to clear his mind. At this point in an investigation, the most dangerous thing was to pursue the obvious course of action without considering other possibilities. He thought about Thomas and her confederates. If they were the men who killed Stevens, they were professionals. They were comfortable enough to rent a hotel room in Oshawa and willing to quietly check out of the hotel even though one of their team had an RCMP .45 caliber round in his side. They would not be flustered by the revelation that Thomas had been discovered to be a spy. They would have an escape plan, most probably two or three contingencies. He said to Creed, "Where is the closest airfield? I'm sure you use a local field to train your students in air deliveries."

Creed nodded. "We use RCAF Kingston. It's a training base for Canadian pilots, and our training missions are perfect for their students and instructors. It's in Collins Bay just west of Kingston."

Lundin shook his head. "Too far. Any other airfields that you know of around here?"

Creed seemed puzzled, as if he didn't seem to follow Lundin's question. Fleming looked at Creed. He addressed him as if he was addressing a recalcitrant child. "Thomas is a pilot. What better way to escape?"

Lundin nodded. "If she was piloting military aircraft with ATA, she can fly just about anything. I'm not sure this is the right answer, but it certainly would be my answer if I intended to escape."

Creed finally understood. He said, "Before this class started, we looked at the airfield just north of Oshawa. It is another RCAF training station, but they only fly old trainers. Mostly biplanes, Tiger Moths and other aircraft from the Great War."

Fleming added, "It was one of our first recce challenges. We scouted the perimeter and took photos of the aircraft. It was the first time I worked with Thomas. She was very interested in the recce."

Creed nodded. Lundin and Fleming were already running to the Buick. Lundin shouted over his shoulder, "Stay here!"

They drove away, leaving a cloud of dirt and dust behind them. Lundin didn't slow down as they approached the camp gate. He turned on the police siren as he neared and at the last minute the guards lifted the barrier. Lundin smiled and said to Fleming, "I guess they got the message."

The drive from the camp to the airfield avoided downtown Oshawa. The few vehicles and tractors on the roads pulled over when they heard the police siren and saw the Buick racing toward them. On the drive, Fleming asked, "What did you find in Stevens' room?"

Lundin reached into his pocket and tossed the small package over to Fleming. He opened it to find another silver dollar. "They teach us to have two concealments so that we can pass them back and forth."

Lundin nodded. His face was a grim mask. "Stevens never got a chance to pass this one."

As they approached the gate to the RCAF station, Lundin slowed. He turned to Fleming and said, "Ian, it's once again time for you to show your skills."

He stopped just short of the barrier. Before the guards could even come out of their small kiosk, Fleming was out the door and shouting. "Gentlemen, I am Commander Fleming, Ian Fleming. I am on a special mission for your base commander. I have already commandeered an RCMP cruiser, and I do not intend to be delayed. Open the gates!"

The RCAF sergeant in the kiosk stood up and saluted Fleming.

He slapped the man next to him and said, "Selkirk, you heard the commander. Open the gate!"

Fleming got into the car, and before he closed his door they were off again, siren blaring.

Lundin said, "Where do we go next?"

"Base operations is that tower building. Just to your right."

Lundin could only see one way to the tower building and that was along the taxiway. He pulled the Buick across several yards of grass and white-painted rocks and then accelerated along the tarmac. Before the car rolled to a stop, both men were out of the Buick, leaving the doors open as they ran to base operations.

An RCAF officer and his two sergeants looked stunned as the two men burst through their doors. One of the sergeants tipped over his small work desk, spilling charts, navigation tools and his tea on the floor. The officer was in his shirtsleeves and trousers. Lundin could not judge his rank and wasn't quite sure how to handle the situation. Once again, Fleming took charge. He said, "Captain, I am Royal Navy Lieutenant Commander Fleming. I work for the Admiralty. My colleague from the RCMP is helping me on a case of utmost security."

Lundin later admitted he had no idea how Fleming pulled off the ruse, but the officer came to the position of attention and said, "Flight Lieutenant Marshall, sir! What can we do to help?"

Fleming smiled and said, "Marshall, we need to know if an ATA officer came to the base earlier today. Flight Lieutenant Thomas. She would have asked if one of your aircraft was available for her to conduct a certification flight before she departed for England."

"Yes, sir! She only arrived about an hour ago. She's down at Hangar 6. None of our training aircraft were ready, so she had to do her safety check and we are fueling it right now. She needs to be quick. There is a storm coming in, and that Tiger Moth won't survive it."

As they ran to the door, Fleming paused for a moment and said, "Good man! You will hear from us."

Once back in the car, Fleming said, "We got her!"

Lundin put the Buick in gear and said, "In the Force, we never say that until the villain is in handcuffs."

They accelerated along the taxiway to the row of hangars, each with a large blue number painted on the doors. As they reached Hangar 5, they saw a bright yellow biplane leave the next hangar and head along the taxiway to the active runway. Lundin pulled off the taxiway, drove across the grass median and onto the runway just as Thomas did a quick ground loop turn and faced the biplane into the wind.

Lundin accelerated toward the plane as the aircraft started its own acceleration for takeoff. Fleming shouted, "Are you going to crash into that plane?"

"Only if Thomas chooses not to stop!"

Fleming braced his hands against the metal handle of the glove box. Lundin thought for a moment that it would end badly for the Buick as he raced towards the biplane. They might stop Thomas, but would they survive the crash?

As it turned out, that wasn't how it happened.

CHAPTER TWENTY-ONE — ENDGAME

Thomas turned out to be an exceptional pilot. Rather than hit the Buick, she lifted the biplane off the ground just above the car, hitting the roof with the wheels of the plane, and then bounced back on the runway. She accelerated and took off. The aircraft did a quick circle of the airfield. Fleming told the admiral later that he was certain she waved as she passed over them and headed toward Lake Ontario. Lundin stopped the car and got out. He was angry at himself and, most importantly, at Thomas. A murderer and spy had escaped justice.

As Fleming got out of the car, they heard a loud bang. Fleming said, "What was that?"

Lundin knew the answer. "It was a rifle shot."

Lundin pointed at the Tiger Moth. Oily smoke was coming from the left side of the engine compartment. Seconds later, they heard another shot. The propeller of the biplane stopped, and the aircraft stalled. The tail drooped while the right wing dropped at an extreme angle. The plane lost lift and slid out of the sky. Lundin was the first to react. He jumped into the Buick, did a quick U-turn and drove down the runway. Three RCAF jeeps, an ambulance and a firetruck followed, speeding in the same direction as the Buick. Before any of the vehicles could reach the end of the runway, a large fireball erupted in the woods off the runway. The biplane was down for good. Everyone watching knew the pilot would not survive.

Lundin and Fleming were first to the crash site. They ran through the pine woods following the sound and the smell of the fuel explosions. Fleming tried to approach the aircraft, but the mix of fuel and the fabric and wood of the biplane were now a conflagration that was scorching the ground and setting the closest trees on fire. Lundin saw Thomas crawling away from the aircraft. Lundin walked slowly over to her, pulled his revolver from his holster and said, "Beatrice Thomas, I am arresting you in the name of the Crown for the murders at STS 103 in the vicinity of Oshawa, Ontario. Please do not make any moves or I will shoot."

Thomas looked up at Lundin. Her face was covered in a mix of oil and blood from a gash just below her flying helmet. Next to her left hand was a military .45 automatic. She said, "I suspect you wouldn't shoot someone who is on the ground."

"Miss Thomas, if you touch that weapon I will shoot you whether you are running, standing or crawling. I want to see both of your hands. Put them on the ground in front of you and do not move."

She smiled and said, "You know they are out there with a rifle."

"I know they are, but they are also smart enough to know that there are plenty of armed men on the way. They aren't dumb. They will assume you died in the crash."

While he had no pity for Thomas, who had killed at least one man (probably two) and was involved in the death of a third, he was glad to see her alive. They would finally know the answers to the entire story. He pulled a set of handcuffs from a leather pouch on the back of his Sam Browne belt and placed them on Thomas' out-stretched wrists.

The arrival of the ambulance and the firefighters brought Lundin back to the immediate present. He turned to a man who demonstrated he was in charge of the fire brigade. He said, "Sir, my name is Senior Sergeant Lundin of the Mounties. When you finally put out the fire, I want to inspect the wreckage. This is a crime scene. Please preserve what you can of the aircraft. I have the pilot in custody." The fire chief nodded.

As he turned back to look at Thomas, he saw Fleming standing above her with his .38 pistol aimed at her head. Fleming pulled the hammer back on the pistol and shouted, "Why Jovanovic? What did he ever do to you?"

Thomas looked up at Fleming and said, "In this shadow war, men die."

"But who are your masters? Moscow? Berlin?"

Thomas softened her voice and said, "Ian, you need to look closer to find my master. You need to look among your own kind."

Lundin ran over to Fleming. He wondered if Thomas wanted Fleming to shoot her. "Ian, we need to know the entire story. If you put a bullet in her head, we will never know the truth. Novak, Jovanovic and Stevens all deserve the truth. Now, put the gun down."

From behind him, the senior fireman said, "Sergeant, I'm focusing on putting out the fire before we end up losing some of this forest and, perhaps, the air station. If there is anything left when we accomplish that mission, it's all yours."

Lundin nodded. Fleming seemed to calm down as Lundin approached. Fleming put away the pistol and Lundin pulled Thomas to her feet. He was not gentle as he pulled her upright. She winced as she put weight on both of her legs. He could see one foot was at a completely unnatural angle. Broken leg, or perhaps broken ankle. Lundin thought to himself that at least she wasn't going to run away.

Fleming walked next to Lundin as they dragged Thomas toward the Buick. "I wouldn't have shot her."

"Wouldn't have?"

"It was a close-run thing." He looked at Lundin. "Miles, who shot the plane?"

Lundin said, "I think her colleagues wanted to end their ties to this entire affair. Honestly, I suspect the camp commander and the HYDRA chief will want that as well."

Fleming shook his head. "So, Thomas will be prosecuted for murder?"

Lundin said, "I leave that to the Crown prosecutors. You and I have captured the murderer. It's all up to them now. You have other things to do, including winning this war. Don't worry, the RCMP will get the answers."

CHAPTER TWENTY-TWO — FAREWELLS

Lundin and Fleming met later that afternoon for one last drink. They had checked out of their rooms. Lundin reported the arrest to the chief inspector and turned Thomas over to the local constabulary to be held for the Crown prosecutor. He intended to drive back to Toronto and sleep in his own bed.

Lundin was drinking coffee, Fleming had bourbon. Lundin said, "I understand the camp commander arranged a late afternoon flight for you from RCAF Kingston to Halifax. I guess you will catch a flight from there to Britain."

Fleming smirked. "They want to see the back of me. I'm not sure if I will be flying or catching a berth in a Royal Navy cruiser. I suspect the camp commander would prefer the latter so a German submarine can send me to the bottom of the Atlantic."

Lundin shook his head. "I doubt that. After all, we closed the case and plugged a leak in HYDRA with little in the way of public attention. Will you fly back with Creed and the other students?"

"Possibly."

"So, all is forgiven."

"Miles, you clearly don't understand Brits. There may be no public attention, but there will be reports that I will have to file and possibly an SOE internal investigation. It won't be pretty."

"Ian, I want you to know that it has been a pleasure to work with you."

Fleming tried to suppress a grin. "That's a lie."

"Well, it has been a productive relationship, and if you are ever in Toronto count on me to host you for a fine dinner and a glass of bourbon or three!"

"Well said! The same goes for me. If you are ever in London, I will be happy to host you. And, I promise, it won't be at some stuffy Royal Navy mess. I have membership in a club that is not in the least bit stuffy."

"They will allow in a Canadian Mountie?"

Fleming laughed. "Only as my guest."

"Then it will be my pleasure."

Fleming turned serious. "Miles, I want you to know that this was a true adventure, and I learned more than you can possibly imagine. I hope you have great success."

Since the Great War, Lundin had never been one to express his emotions. Too many lost opportunities with mates. He didn't know how to respond, so he waved to the bartender and said, "Two whiskies, please." When the whiskies arrived, he raised his glass and said, "To great success!"

Fleming raised his and responded, "And far less supervision!"

The Investigation: Day 12
Closing the file

22 October 1942, RCMP, Toronto

CHAPTER TWENTY-THREE —
THE GAME CONTINUES

Lundin sat at the breakfast counter at St. George's, nursing his second cup of tea. His breakfast plate was empty, and he was enjoying the quiet before walking to headquarters.

Deke limped up to the counter. "So, you saved Canada…again?"

"Well, for once the answer is yes. At least that's what I think."

"No more doom and gloom, then?"

"You know, Deke, it is a strange world. Since the Great War, I have spent my life bringing villains to justice. Suddenly, I had to explore a world where it was hard to sort out allies from enemies, villains from heroes. This new world we are facing isn't going to be all that easy for any of us."

"As if the old world was all that easy? A world war, the flu, the Great Depression, and now another world war?"

"Deke, I just visited a shadow world where there wasn't any black and white, only grey. I think we will be in a shadow war even after we win this one."

Deke looked at his friend as if for the first time in ages. He said, "Well, Miles, welcome back to the real world. I for one am glad you made it back safe and sound."

Lundin looked at his Elgin watch. It was time for work. He said, "Trust me, Deke. I'm happy as can be to be back in the real world." He pulled out a ten-dollar bill. "Keep the change, my friend."

"I'll save it for a bump and a beer the next time we meet."

Lundin looked over his shoulder as he pulled on his rain slicker. "Count on it!"

Lundin sat the conference room at RCMP headquarters in Toronto. The conference room had a series of casement windows facing Lake Ontario and the various government and corporate buildings along the shoreline. It was a typical late-October day in Toronto, with a mix of sleet and rain lashing the windows. For once, Lundin was happy to be inside. The promise of a cold, wet winter was not a welcome thought. He knew that along with all the Mounties in the RCMP, he would be expected to do his duty regardless of the weather. In his small house on the edge of the city, he had already pulled out his wool sweaters, his long underwear and his heavy blue serge wool coat and bright yellow rain slicker. Even inside the headquarters with its inconsistent steam-radiator heating, he usually opted for what he considered his winter uniform — heavy wool trousers, wool shirt and a thick wool sweater.

Unfortunately today was a formal briefing, so the winter kit stayed in his office. Instead he was wearing his tunic over a white shirt and tie. Lundin wasn't entirely sure if it was his age, the clothes, or his disposition, but he was cold. He needed another mug of tea, but that would not happen until he was finished in the conference room. The long, polished maple table had twelve chairs. He knew his place at the table. He was in the center of the table with his back to the windows. The chief inspector would sit directly in front of him facing the windows, with the sergeant major on the chief inspector's right and the visitor on his left.

This was the final briefing for the RCMP murder investigation at Camp X. Once completed, Lundin would close the file. The Crown prosecutor already had their own copy. A mix of prosecutors and Canadian Army officers were continuing their interrogation of Thomas. His copy of the file would go to the archivist in the basement.

After that, he expected to receive another case which would take him out into the Ontario cold. The Oshawa murder file was nearly three inches thick, with biographic information on the three victims and on Beatrice Thomas; detailed forensic information on the Tiger Moth and other evidence collected in the investigation; and, at the top of the file, his summary of the case.

Chief Inspector McClellan walked in. Sergeant Major Tyle followed him. Lundin was already standing at attention when he realized the third individual was RCMP Commissioner Stuart Wood. Lundin had never met the commissioner. While Lundin was usually unimpressed with the protocols demanded when speaking with politicians and other government seniors, the RCMP was his family and he knew that he needed to be on his best behavior in this briefing. He was exceptionally glad that he changed into his full uniform, regardless of the cold.

The three RCMP seniors sat down and McClellan said, "Miles, take a seat and relax." The chief inspector smiled and continued, "I promise, this is not going to be an interrogation." Lundin looked over at Tyle. The sergeant major's normal stern demeanor was less grim than usual, but it was clear he was as nervous as Lundin. One of the office staff knocked on the door and pushed in a formal tea cart with the RCMP office china, a silver teapot and a tray of pastries. He served the commissioner and the chief inspector. Tyle waved him off, as did Lundin. The last thing Lundin wanted was donut crumbs on his chin or his uniform as he tried to explain the case.

McClellan opened the discussion. "Miles, we have all read your preliminary report. The commissioner followed the investigation from the beginning, and we both wanted to thank you for handling a very sensitive case. We even received a formal letter of thanks from the Camp X commander, the HYDRA chief and Mr. Stephenson. Well done!"

Lundin waited for a moment to see if the chief inspector intended to add something. When he didn't he said, "Sir, I did what I could to sort out the case. I'm sorry I didn't get it solved before the last murder, but in the end, the case was resolved."

Commissioner Wood spoke for the first time. "Senior Sergeant Lundin, your efforts were exemplary. I am perfectly satisfied that your resolution of the case was in the highest standards of the Force. As George said, we have received a series of thanks from several seniors in the Canadian and British governments. Of course, the sensitivity of the case is such that it has been handled in the most restricted of channels."

McClellan nodded and said, "Miles, please provide a summary in your own words."

Lundin noticed Tyle, who gave him a look that said, "Well, get on with it!" While he had prepared a detailed report for this conference, Lundin decided to provide a short summary and then ask for questions.

"Gentlemen, the origins of this case are in espionage. We now know that there was a conspiracy at STS 103 involving a Soviet sympathizer at the HYDRA facility, Ken Stevens; a student in the SOE training program, living under the name of Beatrice Thomas; and an unknown trio of perpetrators who we believe were assigned either temporarily or permanently to the new Soviet mission in Ottawa. The murders of the three Canadians, Novak, Stevens and Jovanovic, occurred due to an unraveling of the plot. We still do not know if Thomas is a Canadian, or even if Thomas is her real name. There are no records of her life before returning from the Spanish Civil War and taking her pilot's certification. What is clear is she served as a courier for the espionage plot and may have been the person who recruited Stevens."

Lundin paused to see if there were any questions. When there were none, he continued, "We do not know for certain who shot at her aircraft as she tried to escape. My own suspicion is that other collaborators wanted to end contact with Thomas…permanently. However, that is entirely my conjecture." He paused to see if there were any questions — and whether his bosses were about to throw him out of the room for making such grave accusations against an ally in the war against the Nazis.

Wood said, "Please continue, Lundin."

"Sir, I have established a basic timeline of the events." He handed typewritten sheets to Wood, McClellan and Tyle. "I do not know the origins of the conspiracy. It seems clear that Stevens was already a sympathizer, if not a full agent, of the Soviet Union when he arrived at HYDRA. In my two interviews with Stevens, he made no secret of both his support for the Soviet Union and his despair over the death of Novak. For this reason, I think Stevens likely already had contact with Canadian communists or possibly Soviet agents by the time he arrived at HYDRA. Stevens ran the day shift at HYDRA and, based on the paperwork that Commander Fleming found on Stevens' body, it appears he was regularly passing full transcripts of HYDRA material to Thomas. Novak does not appear to have been part of the conspiracy. Instead, I believe he became suspicious of Stevens after he found a concealment device that Stevens mislaid. It had a map and a code list inside the device. Novak followed the map, came upon Thomas waiting for her contacts and died at Thomas' hands."

McClellan asked, "Miles, what makes you think it was Thomas who committed the first murder?"

"Sir, I will admit this is what I think as opposed to what I know. We have an eyewitness who saw Novak and Thomas walking toward the water just before the murder. We know for certain that Thomas was part of the conspiracy. And, I have reporting from the coroner, one of the instructors at the camp, and from Commander Fleming that the murder could easily have been committed by a woman who received close combat training at the camp. I do not have conclusive proof that Thomas committed the murder. She may have simply lured Novak to his death, but I have no evidence that suggests an outsider was at the camp that night. I hope that she will reveal her role in the conspiracy during subsequent interrogations."

Wood nodded. "Continue."

"I was fortunate to have Commander Fleming as an unofficial

partner in this investigation. Due to his Royal Navy rank and his role as Admiral Godfrey's aide, we were able to gain additional information about several of the individuals involved in the case. I believe Stevens was completely distraught over the death of Novak. After all, Novak was his close colleague, lived across the hall from him and was a loyal and, it turns out, heroic Canadian. Stevens may not have recognized his work with the Soviets was treason or, for that matter, that the conspirators would use violence to protect the HYDRA reporting. I can only guess that Stevens was about to reveal the entire conspiracy in our next scheduled meeting. He was killed by a professional team."

Wood asked, "And not Thomas?"

"Sir, I was investigating Stevens' quarters when I discovered his body and was attacked by a man who used a silenced weapon. I returned fire. He and two other men made good their escape by boat. Later, I recovered a .22 caliber bullet from the door of Stevens' quarters."

McClellan said, "Miles, the man that shot at you died in hospital in Ottawa. He was listed as a clerk on temporary assignment to the Soviet mission. His colleagues reported that he was shot by an unknown villain on the streets of Toronto. The coroner recovered a .45 bullet from the clerk. The Toronto City police could find no evidence of this altercation in Toronto, nor have they found any weapon."

Wood said, "Samuel Colt is attributed to have said never send a man when you can send a bullet. We are confident that your shooting was justified and equally confident that the terrible crime in Toronto will never be solved. Please continue."

Lundin expected more of a challenge to this portion of the report. After the commissioner's comment, he relaxed slightly. "The murder of Jovanovic remains the only puzzle left. I suspect Jovanovic may have witnessed some connection between Thomas and Novak or Thomas and Stevens. My interview with him was brief, and I came away with the impression that he was a loyal Canadian. I believe, but can't prove, that Thomas killed Jovanovic during their final exercise at STS 103. Perhaps Jovanovic saw something that Thomas was certain would reveal the conspiracy. Whatever the cause, it was the final reason why she fled. I do not think Jovanovic's murder was planned, and I don't think any outsider killed him. Again, I hope our interrogation of Thomas will reveal the truth."

Tyle spoke for the first time. "Any evidence to argue that an outsider didn't kill him?"

"The only evidence we have is the fact that Thomas was carrying a .45 automatic when I arrested her next to the wreckage of the Tiger Moth. The weapon was damaged, but I believe our forensics teams will show that this is the murder weapon."

Wood said, "You said you performed forensics related to the aircraft crash."

"After we detained Thomas, I had the firefighters help me recover the engine of the aircraft. With the help of RCAF mechanics, we found two rifle rounds in the engine block. They were both 12.7mm rounds, very similar to our own .50 caliber rounds used in RCAF aircraft and used as anti-aircraft and anti-personnel weapons on our Sherman tanks. I checked with our armorer, who checked with the SOE armorer at the camp. He said the Soviets use a heavy rifle with that caliber for long-range anti-tank and sniper operations. The RCAF helped me search the forest area. I never did find any cartridge casings."

McClellan looked at Wood. The commissioner said to Lundin, "I think we have a good idea of the case. Once again, thank you for your diligence."

Lundin said to McClellan, "Sir, I look forward to serving as a witness in Thomas' trial. In the meantime, I will take the file down to the archives."

McClellan smiled. "Miles, you will not be a witness in any trial. STS 103 and HYDRA are secure. Only the four of us inside this room, and perhaps Room 39 in London, need to know the full story. The Crown prosecutor's officer along with colleagues from the British Security Service have decided that Thomas will be transferred to

England for further interrogation and detention. The government has no interest in making a case against our current Soviet allies."

Wood said, "Sergeant Lundin, I hope you understand that from the perspective of the Force and the Dominion, this investigation never took place."

McClellan held out his hands. "Miles, please pass me the file."

Lundin was puzzled by this. Once completed, all investigations were always archived. One never knew when a case might need to be revisited. He handed the file over to his commander.

The commissioner took a sip of tea and said, "Miles, now that this case is completed, I have an offer I would like to make."

Lundin had no idea how to respond, so he simply said, "Sir."

"The Force needs experienced men who have demonstrated an ability to conduct sensitive operations. I heard directly from Admiral Godfrey that Commander Fleming thought you were a good candidate for what our British colleagues call counterintelligence operations. Mr. Stephenson at the British Security Coordination office echoed that sentiment. We have been working counter-espionage operations since the beginning of the war and did the same in the last war. But modern counterintelligence operations require a more proactive effort to find enemy agents, as well as Canadians who might be collaborators with those agents. I am building a small cadre inside the Force who will be working against any foreign intelligence officers living in Canada or travelling through Canada. I repeat, any foreign intelligence officers. I would like you to join that cadre. You would remain assigned to George's staff, but your work would focus exclusively on this new counterintelligence mission. You will be working on future cases that will never exist in the files of the Force. Is that clear?"

Lundin looked at Tyle. He offered a very slight nod. He looked at the chief inspector. McClellan said, "Well, say something man! The commissioner just offered you a job."

Lundin nodded and said, "Sir, I would be most honored to take on this new challenge."

Wood stood up. McClellan, Tyle and Lundin followed. The commissioner said, "Well, that's all good."

Wood and McClellan left the room. Tyle said to Lundin, "Miles, you are certainly in the shit now. Non-existent files, villains that disappear before trial and orders coming directly from the commissioner to work on cases that don't exist."

Lundin nodded. He said to the sergeant major, "I think I will have some tea and a donut now."

"Always a good choice."

NOTES

This novel is based at a real UK-US-Canada special operations training facility known as STS 103 or Camp X. Camp X was created through a partnership of William Stephenson and William Donovan. As described in the novel, Stephenson was a highly decorated Canadian aviator in WWI who made a personal fortune in the interwar years and served as the head of the British Security Coordination in New York. His telegram address was Intrepid. While initially he served as a representative of the British Secret Intelligence Service (SIS aka MI6), by 1941 he served as the North American representative for SIS, the British Security Service (MI5) and the Special Operations Executive. He was also a close contact with William Donovan, an American Medal of Honor recipient in WWI. Donovan served as the "coordinator of information" (COI) from June 1941 until July 1942, when he became the commander of the Office of Strategic Services (OSS). Donovan used COI funds to help build STS 103. It opened the same week that the US entered the war.

HYDRA was a real part of the Camp X facility, and the description of the communications network is based on my research. With regards to all of the physical descriptions of the camp, I am indebted to the extensive lifetime effort of Lynn Hodgson. His books and personal research made this novel possible. The best overall work on how Camp X fit into the larger world of Allied special operations in WWII was written by the UK special operations historian David Stafford. As to SOE training, I based my descriptions on the declassified and published SOE training manual for selection courses both in the UK and at STS 103.

For those not familiar with his writing, including the James Bond novels, during WWII Ian Fleming was a Royal Navy lieutenant commander working as the aide to the Director of Naval Intelligence (Admiral Godfrey in 1942) based out of Room 39 in the Admiralty. Fleming was a very close contact of Donovan and did receive a revolver from Donovan engraved "for special services." Fleming did visit and participate in training at STS 103 in the fall of 1942. In reviewing the various Fleming biographies, I was unable to confirm the specific dates when he trained at STS 103. I simply picked dates in mid-October because his biographers have provided details of other travels before September 1942 and during December 1942. The most recent biography of Ian Fleming, written by Nicholas Shakespeare, was not available in the US when I finished the novel. Mr. Shakespeare may have identified more information.

Senior Sergeant Lundin is a fictional character. He is an amalgamation of my few direct contacts with members of the Force and my long-standing admiration of the RCMP. Lundin's direct supervisor Chief Inspector McClellan and the RCMP Commissioner Wood are real individuals who served in their positions during WWII. I have done my best to provide an accurate portrayal of these two giants in the RCMP pantheon. Any errors related to the portrayal of the RCMP are entirely unintentional.

Soviet espionage in Canada began almost as soon as the Soviet mission opened in Ottawa. In fact, the first real breakthrough in both Canadian and US counterintelligence operations against the Soviets occurred following the defection of a Soviet intelligence officer assigned to Ottawa. The defection of the GRU cipher clerk Igor Gouzenko in 1945 revealed the extensive efforts on the part of both the Soviet security service, or NKVD, and the Soviet military intelligence service, or GRU. The RCMP Intelligence Branch played a central role in the subsequent investigations in Canada. In this story, I have simply imagined that the RCMP had earlier insight into the Soviet espionage threat.

While this novel is in no way an effort to re-write history, I hope it opens a window into the annals of special operations in North America and sends the reader in search of the real history, which has been chronicled by historians in North America and in the United Kingdom.

J.R. SEEGER is a western New York native who served as a US Army paratrooper and as a CIA case officer for a total of 27 years of federal service. In October 2001, Mr. Seeger led a CIA paramilitary team into Afghanistan. He splits his time between western New York and central New Mexico.

Seeger is the author of the MIKE4 series of eight novels featuring US Special Ops forces and the Steampunk Raj series of spy adventures for younger readers.